Prisoner of the Harem

By G. H. Teed

Illustrated by Eric Parker

First published in the Union Jack magazine,
New Series, No. 1471, 26 December 1931.

Stillwoods Edition

Stillwoods.Blogspot.Ca

A Complete Story of Sexton Blake and G. M. Plummer.

of the HAREM

By G. H. TEED

"Come on, you gutter rat! Spill what you know, or I'll see that you take a journey to Devil's Island."

It was a wonderful scheme; better than silver, better than gold, better than diamonds—just as George Marsden Plummer told his partner Vali Mata-Vali. Hardly any risk either, and almost legal! But somehow things went wrong. Sexton Blake happened to be in Cairo too.

Catalogue Information:
Title: Prisoner of the Harem
Author: G. H. Teed (1886-1938)
Illustrator: Eric Parker
First published in the Union Jack magazine, New Series, No. 1471, 26 December 1931.
This Edition by: Stillwoods, 2023
ISBN Canada: 978-1-998819-05-8
Blog: Stillwoods.Blogspot.Ca
Author Blog: http://ghteed.blogspot.com/
Storefront: http://www.lulu.com/spotlight/lulubook22

https://tinyurl.com/ve25d42s This link should go to a spreadsheet of all known Teed stories. The list is annotated with various information on the stories and my progress with recapturing the work. The library of Teed's stories increases almost weekly. Check at the Lulu.Com for the latest arrivals. Search for Teed. /drf

Keywords: Sexton Blake, George Marsden Plummer, Egypt

Cautionary Note: This series of books by Stillwoods are intended to make the stories of G. H. Teed, born in New Brunswick, Canada, available to collectors and researchers. The editor, or rather digitizer has not altered the original publication.

This story may contain language and racial terms that are not appropriate to today. I apologize for them; I know that the author was using his voice to excite and entertain an adventurous English audience. These works were published from 82 to 110 years ago. Most every work has characters of redeeming ethnicity within.

I hope you enjoy and share these stories; I have.

Doug Frizzle

Sexton Blake, Detective, in a tense drama of underworld intrigue and peril in modern Cairo. Story features also George Marsden Plummer, is Complete in this issue and —For readers of all ages.

It was a wonderful scheme; better than silver, better than gold, better than diamonds —just as George Marsden Plummer told his partner Vali Mata-Vali. Hardly any risk either, and almost legal! But somehow things went wrong, Sexton Blake happened to be in Cairo too.

Al Muski

GEORGE MARSDEN PLUMMER paused before the small, somewhat dingy window of the antique shop and scrutinised critically the diamond-set ornament that winked at him in a slanting ray of sunlight.

He had recognised it at first glance. He ought to have done so. It had once been in his possession. Indeed, so intimately had he regarded it and so carefully had he guarded it, that he had carried it in a little chamois bag slung round his neck.

It had come into his possession in the same way he usually acquired such valuable trifles —by a slick bit of stealing. And, struck by the exquisite beauty of the filigree setting as well as by the wonderful purity of the square-cut rose diamond, he had determined to hang on to it as long as possible.

He knew that, when the time did come to dispose of it, he would receive from any fence only a small fraction of what it was really worth. It was the sort of stone which, even if prised from its setting, would be known to most of the big international jewel dealers.

As a matter of fact, he had disposed of it in Paris for exactly one thousand pounds, which, since he was hard pressed for money at the time, seemed a satisfactory enough figure.

That was more than a year ago. Now here was the same piece, apparently untouched, lying in the window of a small antique shop in Cairo. How did it come here? What was its history since he had surreptitiously passed it over to the fence in Paris?

Plummer's curiosity was strong, but not sufficiently so to lead him into making any rash move. Yet, as he sauntered on along the narrow street, he was thinking fast.

He knew positively that it was the same piece that he had "lifted" from a certain Englishwoman, the wife of a rich manufacturer. Whether she had ever reported the incident to Scotland Yard he did not know. There had been certain conditions surrounding that little affair which she might not wish to broadcast —incidents cunningly contrived by himself. In that case, he had told himself at the time, he was safe enough.

On the other hand, if her husband discovered the loss there might be some awkward questions. He hadn't dared take any risks. So he had held the thing against a more opportune moment for disposal, had seized that moment when necessity drove, and here was the jewel in Cairo.

How had the antique dealer got hold of it? Who was he, anyway? Of what nationality? Was he a native Egyptian —Copt or Syrian or Arab —such as were scattered throughout Cairo, doing a thriving trade in fake antiques with foreign tourists? Did he know the value of the rose diamond that seemed to have been dropped so carelessly into a tray along with lesser baubles? Or was there something deeper behind it?

If this latter were the case, then he would try to ferret it out. Heaven knew he needed badly enough to get his fingers on some money. Since a recent and most disastrous affair in Morocco, he had been up against it badly. Ever since he had got away from Ben Souki by the skin of his teeth —he and Vali Mata-Vali —things had been about as bad as possible.

He shuddered when he remembered how they had come along the North African coast in a vermin-ridden dhow, to be dumped into Alexandria like so much cargo; when he remembered the futile efforts there to turn a trick and get hold of some real money; of the hot, dusty journey from Alexandria to Cairo, and of the lean days since arriving there.

By dint of many expedients he had managed to keep up a fairly respectable appearance.

Yet he kept away from the big thoroughfares like the Boulevard Mohammed Ali, the Muski, and the Great Nile Bridge that takes one across to the island of Gezira Bulak.

It was, in fact, because he was avoiding the Muski on his way into the Oriental City that he had chanced to pass the small antique shop in the narrow street. And now, while he pondered on the surprising thing he had seen, he took care not to pass the corner.

He paused close to a *sebil* (public fountain) at one corner and lit a fresh cigarette. These cost little enough, thank goodness. He was trying to figure out some reasonable explanation of how that lovely rose diamond came to be where it was.

He was quite oblivious of the constant procession of horses, camels, asses, and human beings that crowded and jostled him; of the bulging upper stories of the rickety old buildings that nearly met overhead, almost shutting out a view of the intensely blue sky; of the brilliant colours of the curious garb worn by the amazing conglomeration of nationalities that pushed into or out of the stream— cunning-witted Cairenes, bedouins from the desert, fellaheen from the country districts, negroes and Nubians, Armenians, Syrians, Copts, Jews, and Franks, not to mention every European race on the map. Oblivious also to the shrill cries of the dirty but picturesque sellers of sherbet and fruit, of the apparently somnolent merchant squatting outside his little shop; blind and deaf to a sight that draws all the world, and grips the Westerner as fiercely as the Oriental. For Plummer's mind could function round but one thing just now —that rose diamond in its filigree platinum setting.

He came to a decision suddenly. Flinging away the end of his cigarette, he turned and strode back along the street. He paused for only the fraction of a moment in front of the window of the antique shop, then he stepped into the little entry and opened the door.

Nothing was lost, on entering, of the impression gained from the dusty window. The interior was gloomy, a confusion of rugs and pots, brass and copper, gimcrack trifles. On the left, a row of dirty showcases contained a medley of baubles, from Birmingham-made scarabs to glittering gems that might or might not be genuine. At one end, coarsely woven jute panels, the motif being the ubiquitous Pharaonic, concealed a back shop from which, as Plummer closed the door, someone emerged.

At first he could not see distinctly just what sort of person this was. But presently he could distinguish the frail, bent figure of an old man, his eyes peering short-sightedly through thick-lensed glasses, his fingers combing through the strands of a long, white beard.

And then George Marsden Plummer got a second shock for, if he had been amazed to see the rose diamond in the window, he was even more surprised to recognise the individual before him.

He laughed softly and spoke in French.

"Eh, old stager, what a pleasure to come upon you here in Cairo! What a safe hole for the weasel to hide in! I'll wager I am the first of your old friends to pay you the compliment of a visit."

The old man had stopped in his tracks. But that was the only sign that he was startled. His eyes still peered through the thick lenses; his fingers continued to comb through his beard.

"You speak strange words, monsieur," he said at last in a weak, thin voice. "I do not know you. You wish, perhaps, to see some trifle?"

Plummer laughed again, not quite so gently.

"So that's you're pose, is it, my dear Ferrand. Well, we'll see what we shall see. It takes more than that ragged beard you are wearing to disguise the features of Jacques Ferrand, the slickest fence in all Paris. I wonder how you got that rose diamond from Humbert. And I'm curious to know why you've got it tossed in amongst all that junk in the window. Humbert didn't give you its history, I suppose; didn't tell you he got it from me. Well, it's a banal saying, Ferrand, but true nevertheless; the world is a small place."

He broke off suddenly and, springing forward, caught hold of the other's beard. For one moment it had come to him that, after all, he might be mistaken in thinking this was Ferrand in disguise. He might, he thought, be making a bad break that would react on himself. He would soon settle that point.

There was a yell of pain from the old man as Plummer tugged. His bent form straightened and he shot out hands that gripped Plummer's wrists with amazing strength. But Plummer was not to be deterred. He gave a vicious tug and came away, the long false beard in his grasp. The other's chin was bleeding in two places where skin had come away with it, for it had been affixed firmly. But now there could be no doubt, and while he gazed at the result of his action Plummer laughed again.

"Voila, my old fox!" he jeered. "What have you to say now?"

Ferrand, for it was the notorious fence as Plummer had thought, sprang from his grasp with a furious jump. He leaped behind the counter and snatched up an automatic pistol. He whirled to fire, but before he could do so, Plummer was upon him, had torn the weapon from his grasp and then, despite his frantic struggles, hauled him along to the curtains at the rear. Kicking these aside he revealed a sort of small office. He flung Ferrand into the desk chair and bent over him.

"Now, you squirming weasel, we'll have a little talk," he said.

"WHAT do you wish to know?"

Ferrand's voice was sulky, but it was plain that he was in dire fear of Plummer. The master criminal possessed a hectic reputation in Paris among other crooks as well as among the police.

"Quite a number of things, old-timer!"

He lit a cigarette, seated himself and kept the pistol where he could use it as a club if necessary.

"Firstly, how long have you been in Cairo?"

"Nearly three years!"

"If that isn't a lie, how did you get that rose diamond from Humbert?"

"I have received nothing from Humbert since I left Paris."

"Then how did you get the diamond? Don't bluff that you don't know which jewel I refer to. I'll drag you along to the window and show you if you try anything as feeble as that."

"I do not bluff. I —"

"Wait a minute! You say you have been in Cairo nearly three years. You wouldn't clear out of Paris and lurk here in such a disguise unless you'd got into things pretty hot in Paris. You're deeper than I thought, you old fox, though I always knew you were pretty slick. We'll keep to essentials. There isn't anything of any particular value in that window compared to the diamond I spotted. And I haven't seen much inside the shop. But you've got plenty of stuff tucked away —I'll warrant that.

"It looks as if you and I were going to find each other useful, Ferrand. I need you, and maybe you'll need me before we finish. I'm going to give you a chance. Take me in and I'll turn any trick you want; leave me out and I'll spill to the French Minister where you are to be found."

Ferrand blanched so suddenly that Plummer was amazed. He didn't have the ghost of a notion why Ferrand had left Paris, but he knew it must have been something pretty raw for him to be in hiding in this fashion, as he had said.

But he was too shrewd a judge of criminals and their ways not to realise that Ferrand's crime must have been of a major kind. As a matter of fact he had been out of France for so long that he was not possessed of much gossip of the underworld. And, a year or so before, when Plummer had passed through Paris, he did not spend much time in places where he would hear things. Had he done so he would have learned that Jacques Ferrand had done a particularly revolting murder upon a young girl in his employ.

Yet Plummer was more intrigued than ever to know how the rose diamond had come into Ferrand's possession; and, even more, to understand how it came to be lying out in the window among comparatively valueless baubles. He told himself that this must be for some particular reason.

Suddenly his easy manner changed. Leaning forward he fixed his strange agate-like eyes on those of Ferrand.

"Come on, you gutter rat," he snarled, "spill what you know, or I'll see that you take a journey to Devil's Island."

Again that fearful blanching; then:

"Why do you come here and worry me? I have never done you a harm. In Paris, whenever you brought me things I paid a fair price. I have little money left, but I will give you five thousand francs to go and leave me."

Plummer laughed harshly as he got to his feet. He laid the automatic on the desk and, bending over, caught Ferrand's neck in his powerful hands. He lifted him bodily out of the chair as if he were a chicken; then he hissed in his ear, slowly while he jerked his head back and forth:

"I've told you —no nonsense —you'll fool with me —will you —one more —chance you get —then I —strip this place —before passing the word —to — the French Minister."

He flung the wretch back into his chair and again took up the pistol. He watched Ferrand while he put up a trembling hand and felt his bruised neck. He started to move forward once more, but now Ferrand gave a hoarse cry of terror and strove to speak.

"I —I —I will —tell," he managed to gasp.

"Get on with it then."

"It is there as a signal —a sign!"

"For someone to see?"

"Yes."

"And then?"

"That person will come into the shop."

"This begins to sound interesting. Is that person man or woman?"

"A —a woman."

"European?"

"Yes —an American."

"Still more interesting. Just why does this American woman need such a sign in the window of this dirty hole? And why that particular rose diamond?"

"Because I bought it from her."

"Did she get it from Humbert?"

"I do not know. She bought it openly and honestly in Paris."

"Why did she sell it to you?"

"For the usual reason —she needs money."

"If she is an American woman, stranded here and needs money, why does she go about selling a jewel in such a hole-and-corner fashion?"

"She is not at liberty to dispose of her jewels openly."

PLUMMER'S eyes were very thoughtful as he lit a fresh cigarette.

"Getting information out of you is like pulling teeth!" he said at last. "You'd better tell me the whole story. I may be able to help."

Ferrand's manner had changed a little. During the last few minutes, while he was answering Plummer's questions as slowly as possible, he, too, had been thinking. And now he was telling himself that, after all, it might be a good thing that this crook had turned up. He might, indeed, be able to make use of him, and, incidentally, turn a little more profit for himself. If Plummer succeeded in getting his throat slit —and there was a very good chance of that —so much the better.

"I will tell you all —in strict confidence," he muttered, as if reluctantly. "This lady is indeed Americaine. She is the wife of a very rich Egyptian. They met in Paris, and were married there. At the time of the marriage it was understood that, although he was a Mohammedan by religion, she would not be called upon to live as the women of that religion. She was to be as free to come and go as if she were married to a European."

Plummer smiled cynically.

"I've heard that tale before."

"It is true."

"I can believe it. Let's have the rest."

"Ever since they arrived in Cairo she has been forced to don the veil, just like any Mohammedan woman. She is only allowed out in the care of his trusted servants. She is allowed to go to the opera and the theatre as European women, but only when her husband is with her. And even then she is not allowed to speak to other European or American women. She is Americaine, as I have said, and she is spirited. She finds the situation intolerable, and desires, at any cost, to get free."

"Why doesn't she get word to the American Consul?"

"She has tried to do so, but that is useless. He can do nothing. She is now of Egyptian nationality, and any interference would be most difficult. She has even tried the British —with the same result. Also, she was warned in Paris before the marriage what the result would be; but, like so many women who travel abroad alone, she became infatuated. Also, she tells me, he hopes to get possession of the rest of her money, although she has already given him half her fortune—and he allows her nothing for herself but what he doles out."

"And I suppose she thought she was going to queen it on the top level of Cairene society?" drawled Plummer. "Well, these dames ask for it —and usually get it. But where do you come in, my honest Ferrand? I can't quite picture you as the squire of distressed ladies."

"It was by the accident that she came here. She was driving past in her husband's car, and attended, as usual, by his servants, when she noticed my shop. She did not enter that day, but on another the car was stopped and she entered. The men-servants remained outside, but a woman attendant came in with her. She signed for me to come into the back of the shop —this room —and handed me the diamond which you saw. She begged me to buy it. I refused, until she pleaded so hard that I at last consented."

"I'll bet you knew the diamond, and had the breeze up."

"I had never seen it before."

"Well, what then?"

"She accepted what I offered and went away. But the next day her waiting-woman came to the shop and gave me a letter. This letter told me her story. She begged me to help her. I had told her that I was but a poor dealer, so she besought me to buy more of her things from her to raise money for her to use as bribes in making her escape. If I consented to do so I was to make some signal that she could see in passing. I told the waiting-woman that she should look in the window for the jewel she had sold me. If it was there she would know that I was willing. If not, she must not come here again."

"Why did you need time?"

"I wished to learn what I could about her husband before committing myself."

"You're a cunning rogue, Ferrand. And what did you learn?"

"You know Cairo well, monsieur?"

Plummer grinned.

"As well as I know Paris."

"Then you may know this name." With that, Ferrand leaned forward and wrote a name on a slip of paper, giving Plummer only a couple of moments to read it before he tore the paper to shreds. As for Plummer, he gave a low whistle.

"So that's who she is," he muttered. "Is this straight, Ferrand?"

"It is the truth."

"You're playing with worse than fire there, old man. That bird is one of the powers in Egypt."

"I have learned that."

"Then the potential reward must be pretty large for you to risk your skinny neck. If he caught you at your tricks it would be just like this for you!" And with the words, Plummer drew a finger across his throat.

Ferrand licked dry lips.

"I —I know that, monsieur, but what can one do? I have promised."

"For a mighty big price, I'll wager! Why does she have to bring only one piece of jewellery at a time? Why can't she bring all she's got, cash in, and get away?"

"Because she runs a great risk as it is. He asks her to wear this piece, that piece, at unexpected times. If she cannot produce what he names she must explain."

"That's true enough. This looks like a pretty complicated business to me, Ferrand. How is she going to get away when she gets the money?"

"She thinks she can bribe her way out of the palace, and then she counts on finding one of her own countrymen in Cairo who will help her out of the country. But I have been thinking, monsieur, why should not you be that person? You know Cairo, and its underground ways. In this, as you suggested, it may be that you can help."

"And you take all the profit!" jeered Plummer. "Not for this chicken! I'll sit in on the main game or not at all. How long has that diamond been in the window?"

"Two days only."

"And she hasn't come yet?"

"No. But her coming is uncertain. It will be only when she can manage it."

Both men were suddenly silent as a slight sound reached them from the shop. Ferrand made a gesture of caution, and, rising, moved softly to the curtain. Peering through a slit, he stood motionless for a moment or two; then he signed for Plummer to approach.

Plummer was beside him in a flash. Looking over the other's head, he found he could see right along to the door. And there, standing in the gloom, was a veiled woman.

PLUMMER tapped Ferrand on the shoulder, and motioned for him to pass through into the shop.

He didn't need any telling that this was the woman of whom they had just been speaking. He knew it. And when Ferrand obeyed, and he saw another veiled figure move into view, he guessed easily enough that this must be the servant.

He watched while Ferrand approached the two. Then, just as the taller of the two began to speak in low, hurried tones, he slipped between the curtains and advanced.

Even down the length of the shop he could hear the sudden intaking of breath, as the woman who had begun to speak to Ferrand saw him in the gloom.

And, despite his European clothes and lack of fez, he must have looked like Arab or Egyptian in that light.

His skin was mahogany dark from the sun and wind of the Moroccan desert. His black beard, trimmed and forked like that of a bedouin, was as un-European as possible. Nor is it any wonder, after the long years he had lived in the Riff country back of Morocco as Sakr-el-Droog —Hawk of the Peak.

He lifted reassuring hands, while his teeth showed white against the black of his beard and moustache in a smile.

"You have nothing to fear, madam," he said softly in English. "Ferrand here will tell you that I am a friend. He has asked me to help, and I am ready to do so."

She turned to him swiftly, and laid a hand on his arm.

"Oh, will you indeed do so? Can I trust you?"

"To the death," responded Plummer smoothly. "But we must discuss things, and this place is dangerous. When you have finished your business with Ferrand I will tell you what I suggest. In the meantime I shall stand here in the shadow, so as not to be seen."

He had caught sight of a luxurious limousine at the kerb, with a powerful native footman seated beside the driver. It was plain that this woman's Egyptian husband sent her out well guarded, and Plummer knew how swiftly the plan would be nipped in the bud if those hefty fellows suspected anything. As for the waiting-woman, he could do nothing. That was entirely a matter for her mistress. But as he trusted no native women, he knew that she might only be biding her time to allow her mistress to get deeply incriminated before betraying her.

He drew back into the shadow and watched with keen eyes, while Ferrand's client surreptitiously drew out a long, narrow jewel-case and handed it to him. He guessed that it would contain a valuable necklace, and he could hear the woman whispering:

"I brought this to-day because I wore it last night. He may not ask me to put it on again for some days. But will this not be enough? Time is so precious. If he suspects, I may not be able to come again. Please say it will be enough to give me what money I need."

The pleading and fear in her tones might have roused the latent chivalry of most men, but not so those two rogues. Plummer saw Ferrand snap open the case, and then he brought his teeth down on his lip to bite back the exclamation that almost slipped out.

Even from where he stood he could see that it was indeed a necklace, a priceless, wonderful, lovely thing of diamonds. And because he did not want Ferrand to overplay his hand as well as because he was forming a much deeper and more complicated plan that was intended to put him in command of the game, he whispered:

"It will surely do, madam. I shall see to that. Ferrand will get you a good price for it. And now, come to the back of the place, where I will tell you what I suggest."

She swept him a grateful look above her veil, and crept after him down the shop, leaving the waiting-woman on guard. Once beyond the curtains, she deliberately lowered her veil, and Plummer's eyes glinted in quick admiration as he saw that she was really very beautiful. Quite aside from other reasons, it would be a pleasant bit of business to help her. But he mustn't forget two things —Vali Mata-Vali and the Egyptian husband.

"It is exactly as Ferrand has told me?"

His voice was sympathetic, encouraging. Her reply was eager.

"Yes, oh yes!"

"You would make your escape if you could?"

"If I do not get away soon from this horrible life, I —I will —"

"I think I understand. Will you confide in me your name before you married this Egyptian gentleman?"

"Fortescue —Mrs. Adele Fortescue."

"Ah! I know the name quite well. Your husband was Lomax Fortescue, known as the 'Tin-plate King.'"

"Yes. And you —who are you?"

"It wouldn't help if I told you. Let it go that I may be an adventurer who is willing to take a chance on helping you get away from this country. It will be on a business basis. You can reward me as you see fit."

"I can assure you," she told him earnestly, "that once I am free where I can realise on my own money, I shall reward you handsomely. I am still a rich woman, but while I am bound thus —"

"I know; Ferrand has told me. Now, listen. Are you sure you can trust this waiting-woman of yours?"

"I trust her; she is one of the advanced women, and wants to get away from Egypt. I have promised to take her to America if she will help me."

"That's all right, then. But we must have a better means of communication than this. And we must act soon. Would it be possible for you to engage another woman for your own service —one that I should suggest? Or, would your husband object?"

"I could do that if he were not suspicious."

"The woman I have in mind could act the part perfectly. And if she were installed in the place with you, she could act as a safe go-between. In the meantime, I could fix the details of your escape."

"I will do anything."

"Then I will send her to you to-day, and you can engage her as a personal maid. Your excuse can be that she has London and Paris experience. It is too risky to come here often with those two menservants waiting in the car."

She promised him again, and, a moment later, putting up her veil, passed through the shop like a shadow. When she was gone, Ferrand came behind the curtains.

"What have you done? What have you arranged? You spoke in English, which you know I do not understand."

"I am fixing things to the advantage of us both," Plummer soothed him. "And now let us have a look at that string of sparklers."

FERRAND reluctantly presented the case to him. Plummer opened it, and fingered the scintillating gems with loving caress.

"Beauties, beauties!" he kept muttering. "Worth twenty thousand, if a penny! And I don't suppose you will give her a thousand, you old bloodsucker. Where will you sell them?"

"It would be too risky to try and dispose of them in Cairo. They must go to Paris."

Plummer grinned.

"Just what I was going to suggest, my friend. And since I will be there before you, I will take them. Since this is an honest purchase, Humbert will have to pay well for them. After that you shall have your share, old-timer."

Ferrand lifted his hands in frantic protest.

"You would rob me, rob me!" he wailed.

But Plummer cut him short in startling fashion. Dropping the case in his pocket, he again got his powerful hands on Ferrand's throat.

"Listen, weasel!" he snarled. "One more cheep out of you, and I'll snap your neck just like that. You do as I say in this deal from now on. And if you try any tricks I'll see that Zahmy Bey knows of your little transactions with his wife. You get your share, if you are good; if not —"

He let go his grasp, and Ferrand tottered back against the desk. Leaning there for support, he cast abject eyes at the master criminal.

"Wh-what are you going to do now?" he pleaded.

"When I return here I will tell you what I have done," was all Plummer would vouchsafe to reply.

Once out in the street, Plummer made his way as he had intended going before he spotted the rose diamond in Ferrand's window. Where, before, he had been oblivious to all the life and vivid colour about him, now he cast an approving glance in every direction, even refraining to curse a clumsy donkey-boy who deliberately or otherwise, brushed against him.

Things were looking good once more. Life was looking up. An hour ago he had been railing savagely at Fate and the blows it had dealt him. Now he was telling himself what a piece of luck, an extraordinary streak, that he had spotted that rose diamond. He grinned to himself. There was something, after all, in having an eye for a jewel. And as for Ferrand, he would take good care that the little weasel didn't play any hanky-panky.

Even if he continued on going as he was, he was on velvet. He didn't have to wait until he got to Paris to cash in on the diamond necklace. That had been all eyewash for Ferrand. He knew a dozen international crook exchanges right here in Cairo where he could dispose of a plum piece like that for quite a few thousands —Greek, Levantine, and Jew. It was something to be persona grata in the underworld of every city that counted. And the beauty of it was that, except for Zahmy Bey, there wouldn't be any comeback about the thing. It hadn't been stolen.

Even if Zahmy Bey found out, would he split publicity? Not likely. He was too proud a bird for that. What he might do to his American wife was a different matter. But, before anything could break there, he —Plummer —would have her safely out of the country.

The few thousands he might get for the necklace would come in useful. But that was chicken feed to what he would squeeze out of the woman before he finished.

Mrs. Adele Fortescue! It made him laugh. Everyone knew that old Fortescue, the "Tin-plate King," had left millions, millions! And even if Zahmy Bey had got hold of half, there were still many millions left.

And, once he had her out of Egypt, Zahmy Bey could whistle. He couldn't do a thing. After all, he had gobbled half the money already. He was no better than a darned crook himself. He had married the infatuated creature and then robbed her. If he got hold of the other half, he would most likely pitch her into the back of the harem and take another wife under Mohammedan law. It boiled down to the plain fact that he would be really doing Mrs. Fortescue a great service to arrange her escape. He wouldn't sting her for much —say, a million or so. Even at that she would be lucky. And, if she played up, why, he might even use Zahmy Bey as a sponge to squeeze. It would be worth a lot to Zahmy Bey to get her back. It was the sweetest proposition he had dropped on for a long, long time —the risk was nothing compared to the prize, and not a darned thing the law could grab him on.

It was in this mood of pleasant anticipation that he reached the very heart of one of the smaller bazaars. It was, in fact, part of the Frankish quarter in the Oriental city.

The streets were very, very narrow, and, at night, could be equally sinister.

Overhead the bulging upper stories of the old houses leaned towards each other until only a thin strip of blue sky could be seen.

On the ground level were small shops with goods of every Eastern variety displayed; and outside each sat the proprietor either with eyes closed as if asleep or intoning his monotonous chant. In the road itself one could scarcely pass by, so jammed was it with donkeys, asses, and human beings. It was one of the inner, remote bazaars to which the tourist rarely penetrates.

Into the low, dark doorway of one of these houses Plummer dodged. It was not the first time he had made use of this same house in Cairo, and, although in the Frankish quarter, it was the property of a Levantine with whom he had done business in the past.

Up a flight of very narrow stairs he felt his way, and then, on a small landing, to a door. He entered a small room into which only a faint portion of daylight entered, and there, on a low divan by the slatted window, a woman reclined.

She was in Eastern costume, though unveiled, and it must be said that, although most of her life had been spent in the Occident, Vali Mata-Vali fitted in perfectly with this Eastern setting.

She rose with languid grace as Plummer came towards her. She knew him so intimately that she saw at once something important had happened since he had left her earlier in the day, vowing that he would not return until he had dug up something that would ease their great and immediate need.

He threw his hat aside, took her in his arms, and laughed softly against her scented hair.

"I've struck it, my dear, struck it! Better than silver, better than gold, better than diamonds! A million, at least, Vali. And you've got a part to play. There isn't any time to lose. Sit down while I tell you about it."

The girl was in a state of acute agitation.
Some hitch had occurred. Zahmy Bey sprang
to his feet.

Chapter 3. A Private Appointment.

TWO evenings after that conversation with Vali Mata-Vali, George Marsden Plummer, sat in very different surroundings from those dingy rooms in the Frankish quarter.

He was alone in a luxuriously furnished reception-room in one of the numerous secluded and exclusive villas that occupy the western end of the Muski —that region where are situated massive Government buildings, luxury hotels, and flats that are as modern and expensive as anything in London, Paris, or New York.

And his dress was as much in contrast. Instead of the worn whites in which he had appeared a couple of days before, he was now in full evening dress and spotless linen. His studs and links were set with moonstones; a jewelled French order hung on a crimson silk ribbon round his neck.

The villa was the property of an exiled Russian Grand Duke, and as Count d'Armanande (of the old French aristocracy) Plummer had been welcomed as a tenant by the agents who had the house in their care since the departure of the Grand Duke for the French Riviera. When one is able to put down a very substantial sum in advance not even a Grand Duke is likely to sniff too hard.

Needless to say, Jacques Ferrand had provided the immediate wherewithal for Plummer's move. So far, Plummer had not realised on the diamond necklace. He had started certain delicate negotiations which he expected to come to a head in a day or two. But he was in no hurry —not while he had Ferrand on tap as a banker. And, by now, Ferrand was so convinced that Plummer would pull off the big scheme, that he was almost cheerful in digging up the sums for which the master-criminal made such cool demand.

Plummer hadn't heard a word from Vali Mata-Vali since she had left him the previous afternoon. But he had left a note at the rooms in the Oriental city, couched in cautious terms, which she would find at once on going there, and which would tell her where to find him. But he wasn't worrying about her. Her very silence was proof that she had succeeded in being taken on as personal maid to Mrs. Fortescue.

If it hadn't been that Plummer was anxious to get on with the game, he would have been quite content to let things ride as they were for some time to come.

True, he dared not show himself too publicly, and it was

necessary to avoid such places as Shepheard's and the Savoy. But the absent Grand Duke had left a most excellent cellar, a cabinet of very choice Havana cigars, thousands of the finest Egyptian cigarettes, and no end of books in every language. Moreover, Plummer felt quite secure in his servants, for although there were only three, he had picked them himself in a certain underworld resort where he was well known. All in all, he was quite content, and it only remained now for Vali Mata-Vali to bring her end of things to a head.

It was about ten o'clock on the second evening when there came a tap at the door, and a Greek boy entered. Ordinarily his profession was picking the pockets of tourists out in the vicinity of the great Pyramids, but just now he was as suave and correct as any well-trained house servant.

He spoke in French.

"A lady to see you, monsieur!"

"You have admitted her?"

"Oui, monsieur. She is in the small waiting-room!"

"Bring her here at once!"

Two minutes later, Vali Mata-Vali, veiled, as became a good orthodox Moslem woman, entered. She threw off her veil with a sigh of relief.

"So this is the little nest you found! You've done well, old boy! Give me a whisky and a cigarette. That palace would suffocate me if I had to stay there long. Honest to goodness, I'm sorry for the Fortescue woman!"

Plummer obeyed swiftly. When she had taken a long sip of the drink and he had touched a lighter to her cigarette, he glanced at her inquiringly.

"Everything moves according to plan," she assured him. "That creature, Zahmy, is a beast. I'd be inclined to help her if for no other reason than to do him one in the eye. But there's money there, my dear —plenty of it. And I've worked out a plan. Can you act by to-morrow evening?"

"To-night if necessary!"

"Too soon! Listen! You've got to arrange in some way to get Zahmy to receive you. If you can't manage that by to-morrow evening, we'll have to postpone it until you can. But time is short. He treats that woman abominably. He threatened to-day to take her to his place in the desert and keep her there. This was because she demurred at signing some papers that would give him more of her money. He's capable of anything!"

"So am I!" drawled Plummer. "You'll need your nerve with you! Can you fix up what I said?"

"I'll manage it. Count Robert d'Armanande can do a good many things. I'll see that he gets a letter of introduction to-morrow, with a letter asking him to see me to-morrow evening on a matter of the utmost secrecy and importance. That ought to fetch him. But I can't tell you the exact hour. I can say ten o'clock, but he may make it earlier or later."

"If you can put in a hint of politics it might work. I suspect he is plotting against the Government. That is where the money has been going. But we shall be ready for the moment!"

"How are you going to manage to get past the guards?"

"There is only one guard on duty after seven in the evening. I can settle him all right with my gas pistol. But you'll have to understand the plan of the house, and just how we will come —if we can come at all. Then you will have to have a car waiting, and all that arranged!"

"You leave that to me. I'll guarantee that Mrs. Fortescue is safe inside this joint inside of half an hour after her getaway!"

THEY drew their chairs closer, and for the next hour went over slowly and methodically every step that could be foreseen. When they had finished, Vali Mata-Vali took her departure, and, late though it was, Plummer got busy concocting the two letters that he hoped would gain him a private interview with Zahmy Bey.

He knew that he must leave no trail. He knew also that the interview must be fixed so that no one but Zahmy Bey would see him. How to impress him sufficiently?

He remembered that Vali had hinted that Zahmy Bey was probably mixed up in intrigues against the Government. There was a line there if she was right, and as she had probably got her information from Mrs. Fortescue it must be correct.

Very well. If that were a fact, then it stood to reason that he must be in regular communication with the exiled members of the Anti-Government Party. Who were some of them?

He went over in his mind the names of various Egyptians who, he knew, lived out of the country for the country's good —idling about in Paris, on the Riviera, and in Switzerland.

Fedri Pasha. That was the one. He was practically the leader of the band of exiles, but it were better to strike boldly if at all. And, on further consideration, he decided it would be wiser not to commit anything to paper. He would telephone.

Why not now? If Zahmy Bey were at home he might be able to fix things this very night. Of course, Vali might be able to pull off the thing without any assistance from him. On the other hand, there would have to be some legitimate excuse for having a limousine out standing outside Zahmy's place at that hour of the evening. And one never knew when a hitch might occur.

He crossed to the table that held the telephone instrument. In less than two minutes he heard a smooth voice at the other end of the wire.

"Your name, please?"

The words were in English, but Plummer answered in French.

"I wish to be put through to his Excellency."

"That is impossible without your name, monsieur."

"I cannot give it. The matter is one of the greatest privacy."

"He is expecting your call? I am his private secretary, and have received no instructions."

"I can understand that. I am only arrived from Paris, and have a message for his Excellency's private ear. Will you take that to him? I think he will then speak. Inform him, please, that I shall speak a name to him personally."

"Hold the line, monsieur, and I will take your message."

Plummer smoked frowningly for what seemed an interminable time, but which was, in reality, only about three minutes. Then he tensed slightly as he heard a different voice on the wire, a curt, domineering voice that he knew instinctively must be that of Zahmy Bey.

"What do you wish?"

"Is it his Excellency Zahmy Bey with whom I speak?" asked Plummer suavely.

"Oui, oui. Who are you, and what do you want?"

"I ask a very private and secret interview with your Excellency. I have just arrived from Paris, and I have a most important message from his Excellency Fedri Pasha, which can only be given by word of mouth and into your Excellency's own ear."

Now, if he had made a wrong shot he would soon know. There was a prolonged silence at the other end. Then:

"Where are you, and who are you?"

"I crave your Excellency's pardon for not answering those two questions. It were better not. What I have is of the utmost secrecy. I am charged by Fedri Pasha that every caution must be observed. Would your Excellency see me to-morrow evening?"

Another silence. Plummer knew now that his shot in the dark had hit the target. But it was plain that Zahmy Bey was nervous of committing himself to this unknown.

"Why not to-night?"

The query came so abruptly that Plummer almost jumped.

"It is impossible for me to reach your Excellency this evening, and daylight would be too risky."

"Very well. I will see you to-morrow night."

"A thousand thanks! May I beg that your Excellency will arrange that I may come and go without being seen even by the secretary?"

"What hour?"

"Ten o'clock."

"Do you know my residence?"

"I know the outside arrangement, your Excellency."

"Then you will come to the small door in the eastern wall at ten. I shall open it myself. It communicates with my apartments."

"I shall be there to the moment, your Excellency."

There was a click at the other end, and Plummer hung up with a sigh of relief. He wasn't anxious to prolong the conversation and he was smiling with satisfaction as he rose.

His self-esteem might not have been so exuberant had he known what the next evening was to bring forth.

THE following day was a busy one for Plummer.

His first idea of making a clean getaway was to arrange for a private aeroplane at Heliopolis. But then he reflected that any such departure would necessarily be of a public nature, and very easy to trace.

He decided to employ the big limousine and do the hundred and twenty miles to Alexandria by road; that is, after lying low in the villa for a day, or longer, according to conditions.

Then he had to see Ferrand in order to make sure that he made no fool play. He offered, ironically, to take Ferrand along with him. But at the mere suggestion of coming out of his hole the fence turned grey. He didn't want to trust Plummer to see that he received his share, but there was no help for it.

By nine o'clock that night Plummer had things all set. He was dressed with extreme care, even to the French order, which, of course, he hadn't the slightest right to wear. When he finally left the villa in the Muski and stepped into the car, he certainly presented as distinguished an appearance as any member of the diplomatic service —full evening dress, silk-lined evening cloak of a French type, and opera hat, the cloak thrown open at the neck so as to permit fleeting glimpses of the jewelled order.

The Levantine driver knew just what he had to do. Leaving Muski, he drove past the great Citadel and out in the direction of the old city, beyond which some of the great palaces of the ancient nobility lie. Just to be on the safe side, Plummer had made a surreptitious survey of the exterior of the place during the later afternoon. It was an enormous structure, and over the high wall that bounded it he had been able to glimpse the annexe, with its latticed galleries, that he knew must be the harem quarters.

It looked a difficult proposition to him to get from that annexe into the main building and out to the street without being seen by many servants. But he knew that Vali Mata-Vali must have studied the situation with every care before speaking so confidently, and as he drove along in the darkness, he told himself grimly that if Zahmy Bey were the only difficulty, he would soon take care of him.

The Levantine drew up at the corner where the great wall angled east and south. Between the eastern wall and another high wall that bounded an adjoining estate was a very narrow, sandy lane, wrapped in deep gloom at this hour. It made an ideal outlet for the private comings and goings of Zahmy Bey, for, as he knew now, the door in the wall communicated with the Egyptian's personal quarters.

Leaving the limousine just round the southern bend of the wall, he got out and, after a quick look round, stepped into the darkness of the lane. In the sand his feet made only a soft, slushing sound as he went along, one hand running against the wall, so as to feel for the break where the door would be situated.

He came to it exactly twenty paces down by count. He thought it might be useful to know the precise distance from door to corner, in case he returned on the run.

He stood in the doorway for a brief moment while he made sure that he was ready for quick action if necessary, that his gun was loose in the holster that was strapped in his left armpit. Then he tapped lightly on the panel.

The door swung open silently, revealing absolutely nothing but a cavernous blackness. Thus for the space of perhaps ten seconds; then a blinding light broke in Plummer's eyes.

He stood it without flinching. He knew that behind the electric torch Zahmy Bey was studying him in detail. His only action was to move his shoulders a little so that the cloak fell open more widely, revealing the glittering order that hung against his snowy shirtfront.

The light went out as suddenly as it had flared, and a low voice reached Plummer's ears.

"Enter, monsieur!"

Plummer lifted his foot and made a step forward. He felt the thick pile of a soft carpet. He essayed another step, and then fingers grasped his arm. He was held thus while the door was closed, and then once more the light flashed, revealing a short hall with a door at the far end. At the edge of the light he could make out the shadowy figure of a short, stocky man in evening-dress.

"Follow me, if you please."

He strode along after the other to the far door. Then, as it was swung inwards by his host, he saw a room of such massive luxury that the rooms at the Grand Duke's villa seemed almost shabby by comparison.

There were bookcases lining the walls, an enormous flat-topped desk of some richly carved dark wood, sumptuous chairs and couches, fine paintings, soft rugs, exquisite alabaster light fittings— a room truly fit for a palace.

He followed Zahmy Bey over the threshold and now saw him plainly. He was very dark of skin, and wore a crimson fez —the only Eastern touch to his dress. His black eyes were quick of movement and very shrewd. His lips were thick and sensual; his nose cruel. Plummer could well believe that he was capable of all he had heard. And he realised, too, that he would have to keep his wits about him if he were to fool this man.

But he flattered himself he would be equal to the occasion. His part was to keep Zahmy Bey occupied while Vali Mata-Vali did her stunt; then to take himself off before the alarm was raised. He had figured out the line he would follow, and, unless Zahmy Bey had been playing with him all along, he thought he could get away with it.

The Egyptian motioned him courteously to a low easy-chair.

Plummer bowed and sank into it. His host offered cigars and cigarettes. Plummer accepted a cigarette, but declined a drink. He knew that Zahmy Bey was a Mohammedan by religion, and that the orthodox Mohammedan does not taste alcohol.

Zahmy Bey lit a cigar and seated himself at the big desk. He was facing Plummer, and Plummer noticed that he was between him and the door through which they had just come. But his wits came back to the matter in hand as he heard Zahmy Bey's liquid tones.

"And now, your message, monsieur?"

"We are quite alone, your Excellency?"

"Quite. My secretary has gone to the theatre."

"I come from Fedri Pasha."

"Yes?"

"His message, your Excellency —he is anxious to have a personal conversation with you. There are things which he does not wish to commit to paper, or to the ears of another person. He desires to know if it would be safe for him to come to Cairo. If not, would it be possible for your Excellency to make a brief visit to some point in France or Italy?"

Just what answer Zahmy Bey would have made to those questions will never be known, for at the very moment when he opened his mouth to reply there came a hurried, agitated knocking at a door behind Plummer.

Plummer was alert in a flash. Yet he saw the sudden frown that clouded the Egyptian's face. Zahmy Bey half rose from his chair, then seemed to change his mind and sank back. He shot a quick glance at Plummer, who was now wearing an air of polite inquiry, as if he were mutely asking his host why this interruption when he had been guaranteed every privacy.

"I do not understand," he heard Zahmy Bey mutter; then he switched from French into a torrent of Egyptian Arabic, his voice raised and directed towards the closed door.

It opened while he was speaking. A voluptuously formed young woman stood on the threshold. She was unveiled, which was enough to tell Plummer that she was a servant of some sort.

She was wringing her hands, and was obviously in a state of acute agitation. Plummer knew at once that some hitch had occurred. He knew it better when, after she had burst forth with a few words, Zahmy Bey sprang to his feet.

The girl disappeared. Zahmy Bey rushed to the door, and Plummer came to his feet. For the moment Zahmy Bey seemed to have forgotten his existence. He plunged out through the doorway, and Plummer went after him, his right hand sliding towards his armpit holster as he did so.

He found himself in an enormous hall, lit only by a swinging red light that hung in the distance. He could just see Zahmy Bey and the woman as they ran along over the thick rugs.

He knew it was no moment for hesitation even if Zahmy Bey knew he was following. The crisis he had feared was come, and he must save the situation at any cost.

Then suddenly he saw two other figures at the far end of the hall. He could make out, too, the shadowy outlines of a wide staircase. It must be Vali Mata-Vali and Mrs. Fortescue. They must have come down those stairs. The game was up unless —

The woman servant began to scream. Zahmy Bey was leaping towards the two fugitives, mouthing words as if he were spitting them out one by one. His arms were raised, and Plummer knew the moment he reached the two European women he would begin to manhandle them. Not only would Mrs. Fortescue never get another chance, but Vali Mata-Vali would probably be put out of action. Over his household Zahmy Bey held power of life and death; out by the Dakhla Oasis was his desert stronghold. Once in there they would be immured beyond reach. And gone would be that million.

Yet, to do him justice, in that moment Plummer was thinking more of Vali Mata-Vali than of the million. He raced after Zahmy Bey, his weapon now drawn. But he did not shoot; he did not want to bring hordes of servants on the scene.

As he passed the screaming woman-servant he gave her a push that sent her crashing into the wall. The racket caused Zahmy Bey to stop and turn. Plummer sent a quick word to Vali Mata-Vali; then, as Zahmy Bey, suddenly realising the trap that had been laid, opened his mouth to yell for help, Plummer raised his arm. The heavy steel butt of the automatic caught the Egyptian full between the eyes. It cracked the skull as if it were eggshell. Plummer had not tempered the strength with which he struck. Zahmy Bey went down as if a thunderbolt had hit him.

Plummer saw Vali Mata-Vali running towards the woman-servant, who was lying on the floor, moaning. He saw her hand come up, and heard the faint spurting of vapour from her gas pistol. Then all at once the woman was still.

He grabbed Mrs. Fortescue's arm. She had been standing paralysed by the swiftness of the drama —standing gazing with horror-filled eyes at the prone man on the floor, the inert lump that, a moment before, had been a thing of power.

She yielded to Plummer's pull as if in a trance. She allowed him to rush her along the hall to the door that gave into Zahmy Bey's private library. Vali Mata-Vali followed close at their heels.

Just as they reached the threshold shouts sounded at the far end of the hall. Then the heavy pad, pad, pad, of bare feet, as servants rushed in from several directions.

Plummer pushed the two women through and slammed the door. He knew the servants would be held a few moments by the unconscious man on the floor. But he realised, too, that every second was precious.

He found a key in the lock, and turned it. Then he leaped across the room and opened the door by which he had first entered. Vali Mata-Vali had again caught hold of Mrs. Fortescue. She followed Plummer unquestioningly.

Plummer paused only long enough to snatch the electric torch from a small tabourette where Zahmy Bey had laid it, to switch the key from one side of the door to the other, then he landed in the passage, and, just as he closed the door after him, heard the first sounds of assault on the one across the room.

The torch sent a strong beam of light along the passage to the door that would take them into the lane.

Plummer pushed past the two women, the torch in one hand, his automatic in the other. He gripped both of them in one hand while he unlocked the door. When he had switched off the flashlight he opened the door and peered into the lane. All was silent apparently. He would not have been surprised had some of Zahmy Bey's servants jumped him at this spot.

Vali Mata-Vali pushed her charge through the doorway, and stood waiting while Plummer switched the key again and locked the door. Then he pitched the key high into the darkness, so that it must fall in the grounds of the estate opposite.

Followed the rounding of the corner by three shadowy figures, a quick run to the waiting limousine, into which they vanished. Then the car drew away, and while Zahmy Bey's servants were still standing in the library staring stupidly about them, the car was racing towards the Muski at top speed.

And at three o'clock the next morning Zahmy Bey died without recovering consciousness, without being able to throw a single ray of light on the affair that within a few hours was to be the sensation of all Cairo.

*It was when Blake pene-
trated to the inner room
that he came upon some-
body entirely unexpected—
George Marsden Plummer.*

Chapter 4. In Cairo's Underworld.

MR. SEXTON BLAKE stirred the small cup of thick, black coffee thoughtfully.

The man facing him chewed the end of an unlit cigar and waited with what patience he could muster.

"It isn't easy to see where I can be of assistance to you, Mr. Potter," he said at last. "You know, I have no official standing in Egypt. And this seems entirely an affair for the Egyptian police. I do not think they would welcome any intrusion on my part."

"But, good heavens, Mr. Blake, they are saying that my sister killed her husband before taking flight. I know she never did any such thing, although she had reason enough. Zahmy Bey tossed away at least half of her fortune, and would have gone through the rest of it if someone hadn't bumped him off."

Blake was watching the stream of life that was flowing past the terrace of Shepheard's Hotel, that caravanserai de luxe in the most fashionable quarter of Cairo. He was on his way home by air from East Africa and the Sudan, had stopped in Cairo for a couple of days, and, at Shepheard's, had been approached by an American —William Potter. He informed Blake that he was a brother of Madame Zahmy Bey, and had come to Cairo because he was not satisfied that everything was right with her. Then he told Blake what the detective already knew —that Zahmy Bey had been murdered, and that his wife had taken to flight. The inference was that she had committed the deed.

"It is just because she had strong motive and is missing that rumour fastens the deed on to her," said Blake reflectively. "Why are you so certain that she did not do it, Mr. Potter?"

"Because she couldn't have struck the blow that killed Zahmy Bey. I've seen him, and I know. Only a strong man could have done it. His skull was smashed like an eggshell. And, further, my sister didn't have the nerve. All her life she had a horror of killing any living thing. When we were kids I've seen her almost faint when I brought down a sparrow with my airgun. That is how I know. And that is why I am appealing to you to help me find her and clear her of this charge. You can name any fee you like —anything!"

"Did you know Zahmy Bey personally?"

"No. I was in America when she married him in Paris. I tried to stop the affair by cable. I knew the inevitable result. But he seemed to have hypnotised her. Then, more recently, I found that she had made over more than half her fortune to him, and when I couldn't get any answers to my letters I wrote privately to a business friend in Cairo. From what he was able to tell me I gathered that my sister was being kept in a state of what amounted to forced confinement. Well, that doesn't go with any free-born American woman. So I decided to pop over here and investigate matters. I arrived to learn —what you know.

"At his palace. And I'll tell the world it wasn't easy to get in. Zahmy Bey's secretary, or manager, or whatever he is, turned me down cold, and the police did the same. If you ask me, those birds aren't any too keen on finding out the actual facts. I figure that Zahmy Bey took a hand at plotting against the Government, and privately they're not sorry that someone bumped him off.

"But I'm not standing for the deed to be blamed on my sister. I'm here to find her, to help her, to get her out of this country. I went to the American Consul and got him to pull the strings for me to view the body. The minute I looked at the wound I knew that my sister Adele couldn't have done it. And now I'm at my wits' end. I can't seem to get anywhere with the police. It's like pushing against a feather mattress. Nor can the Ambassador or Consul do anything. She is technically an Egyptian subject, and they can't interfere. But you are different, Mr. Blake, and you are British. Your people have been in this country for many years. You know how to pull the wires; therefore I appeal to you."

Blake felt profoundly sorry for the American. It was obvious that he was labouring under a very strong emotion born of a deep affection for his sister.

It might be, as he said, that she could not, either physically or morally, have struck the blow that killed Zahmy Bey. On the other hand, Blake knew, from long experience, that a desperate woman can rise to extreme heights when driven to the limit. And there was no getting away from the fact that she had vanished —vanished, seemingly, coincidentally with the crime.

Of course, Blake knew no more than what rumour said. There was no doubt that the police were being most reticent about the affair, and he knew there might be real grounds for what Potter had said about Zahmy Bey's activities against the Government.

Blake had known Zahmy Bey by sight —had seen him more than

once on the French Riviera and in Paris. And he had heard it said that the Egyptian was an intriguer of the first water.

"Did your sister know you were coming to Cairo?" he asked suddenly.

He had a reason for this question. It might be, he told himself, that this stocky, middle-aged American business man might have done the deed himself, might have spirited his sister away, and now, while she was getting beyond reach of Egyptian law, was remaining to play a colossal bluff.

"No," came the answer. "I came without saying a word to a soul. I didn't want to give that bird Zahmy Bey a chance to put the bars up against me."

"Do you know who was responsible for the statement that your sister might be guilty?"

"I don't know, unless it was that secretary fellow. At any rate, the police seem to accept it."

"Her disappearance is certainly a bad sign."

"Listen, Mr. Blake! Adele never carried out this job. She had neither the resources nor the initiative. Someone else bumped off Zahmy Bey, and if Adele didn't just manage to grab that chance and run for it, then she has been carried off. I don't profess to know by whom or where. But a man, a strong man, struck that blow."

WHAT man? If Potter was not bluffing, and his deduction was correct, then, again, what man? Was it someone in close connection with Zahmy Bey and his household —in other words, was it an inside job?

If so, then where did Potter's sister come in? Had she been an accessory before or after the fact? Or both? Had she plotted with someone in Zahmy Bey's service to have the deed done and thus effect her escape? She was a rich woman, but it would seem that she had not had much personal control of her money. And it would need a large sum to suborn anyone in Zahmy Bey's service. A powerful Egyptian noble can wreak a terrible vengeance upon any traitorous servant.

If not an inside job, then what outside person had managed to get past Zahmy Bey's guards and kill him in such fashion? How and why had Zahmy Bey received him? Was it a political job? Or was it done in collusion with Madame Zahmy Bey? If the latter were the case, then had she gone from the house with this person? And, if so, whither?

He put several of these questions to the American, but to all of them Potter shook his head hopelessly.

"I can't answer you, Mr. Blake. I've been thinking about that secretary fellow, but I don't believe he had any hand in it. He said, in English, for my benefit, I suppose, that he had spent the evening at the theatre at Zahmy Bey's special request. He doesn't know how his employer used his time. And it struck me that he wasn't any too keen on saying even that much."

"I am not surprised. He and Zahmy Bey's friends may have strong personal reasons for not wishing the police to dabble in the matter. They may prefer to take their own line of inquiry and — vengeance. Do you know if your sister was alone when she went? I mean, did any of her personal attendants go with her?"

"I understand that she went alone. At any rate, I heard of no one else."

"Well, she couldn't very well have walked out of the place and into the streets of Cairo without some definite destination in view. I suppose she really is gone?"

"That's just what I don't know, Mr. Blake. I don't know what happened between her and Zahmy Bey. He may have locked her up in his darned harem, and she may still be there, helpless to communicate with the outside world."

"It is not at all impossible. It seems to me, Mr. Potter, that there is only one place where we might pick up a hint of what has really happened."

"Where?"

"The criminal underworld of Cairo."

"But how could I do that? I wouldn't know where to begin."

"I was just thinking that I might —"

The American leaned forward swiftly and gripped his arm.

"You mean that you will do this —that you will consent to help me?" he begged eagerly.

"I'm not prepared to commit myself to a definite promise," was Blake's cautious reply. "But I am willing to poke about the underworld and see if I can pick up anything."

TO the uninitiated, there are many dingy quarters in Cairo which would seem to present a sufficiently sinister appearance to mask the haunts of the worst denizens of the underworld.

But in most cases they are perfectly harmless bazaars, into which the tourist may stray without the slightest risk of being robbed —other than in the prices he pays for curios, many of which have been made in Birmingham.

On the other hand, there are haunts in the old city where the stranger does not wander about unless accompanied by a trusted dragoman who is persona grata with the inhabitants.

Marseilles has its evil quarter, than which it is difficult to find anything worse. Nevertheless, Port Said can show something even more foul, and Cairo can beat Port Said.

It was into one of these murky warrens of narrow streets and narrower alleys that a rough-looking fellow took his way on the evening of the day when Sexton Blake had had his conversation with William Potter.

Although very swarthy of face, he was not the Arab type. Rather was he of low Levantine appearance, that breed of the lowest which one finds all along the shores of the Mediterranean, and more particularly in the unhealthy haunts of Port Said, Algiers, Tangier, Alexandria, and Cairo.

He was dressed in dirty cotton trousers and jacket, beneath the latter a soiled cotton vest showing. On his unkempt head he wore a battered cap with a cracked peak; on his feet, black canvas deck shoes. He was smoking a cigarette at a "tough" angle, walked with a perceptible roll, and, with hands thrust in his coat pockets and shoulders hunched, had a truculent appearance that one would not be anxious to challenge.

From the first moment of reaching the quarter from the lower end of the Muski he had moved in idle fashion, pausing every now and then before some small shopkeeper's display, criticising the goods in insulting Egyptian Arabic, kicking any stray dog that happened to cross his path, cursing freely the donkey boys and sweetmeat sellers, leering at any woman he encountered, and altogether conducting himself as one looking for trouble.

No one challenged him, not even the tougher residents, who eyed him jealously. Not one of them dared to question his passage, for he carried himself with an air that indicated familiarity with the warren, and as one who was sure of his position. If he proved too truculent, however . . . perhaps later in the night in some dark alley where one could use a knife without risk . . .

But the stranger seemed quite unaware of any possibility of trouble, for he kept on his way, until, at the end of a particularly noisome alley, he came to a short flight of steps that led downwards into a black abyss.

He did not pause. Beneath him were haunts into which only the hardest criminals of the quarter ever penetrated. Down there in that pit was evil that boiled constantly, but rarely broke surface and revealed its lurking place.

The man who plunged into that hole must either be a reckless, ignorant fool, or else must be very sure of what lay beyond.

Whichever it was with this tough-looking Levantine, he withdrew one hand from his pocket, and thrust it out until it touched the wall on his left. Then he began to descend, being swallowed almost at once by the blackness beneath.

He knew there should be fourteen steps before one reached the alley at the bottom. He counted them as he descended; not to check the number, but to be sure of his foothold.

At the bottom he paused for a few moments. Far ahead in the gloom he could see a dull light. Then, without warning, someone brushed past him and padded lightly up the steps. He paid no attention, but he did shift his hand a little, so he could get at his armpit holster in a minimum of time, should it become necessary.

He moved ahead once more, and three times before he reached the closed door above which the lamp hung he felt other fugitive touches as human rats of the place slid by on dark errands of their own.

He paused before the door, but did not knock. There was no need. Almost at once it opened to permit an unveiled woman to emerge —a woman whose forehead was tattooed with a Nubian tribal mark, whose eyes were slumbrous pools of mystery.

She cast black, inviting eyes at the Levantine as they met beneath the light, but, beyond throwing her some familiar pleasantry, he paid no attention, and, with a low, throaty laugh, she walked on, disappearing in the darkness.

But the opening of that door had revealed a strange sight. It did not lead into a house as one might have supposed. Instead, it exposed what seemed to be a very narrow, well-lighted alley. There were tiny houses on each side, through the open windows of which came the light that illuminated the passage. And here were crowds of men and women, passing and repassing as thickly as in one of the outer streets. It was a bazaar within a bazaar.

The Levantine passed through and pushed into the crowd. He paid no attention at all to the houses on each side, so close, indeed, that one's outstretched arms could touch opposite windows. The tinkle of a cracked piano, the lilt of a woman's voice, the deeper rumble of negroes and Nubians and Levantines flowed about him unheeded.

Yet, in any one of the places he could have indulged in any and every form of known vice. His swagger and his persistence carried him straight on through the alley until it turned, and ahead of him was what seemed to be a blank wall. On the right, close to this wall, was another doorway, partially concealed by double half-swing leaves over the top of which he could see into a crowded drinking shop.

The initiated would have known that he had arrived at last at the infamous dive known as "Ali's," a place into which even Ripley Pasha, the English Chief of Police of Cairo, had only penetrated once, and that before the Kingdom of Egypt took over her own police affairs.

The Levantine pushed one of the half-leaves and entered. No apparent notice was taken of him by the motley crowd, but he knew perfectly well that at least a dozen pairs of eyes watched him keenly. Yet he continued as boldly as he had advanced through the bazaar, for Sexton Blake knew that one false move would be his finish.

Chapter 5.　The Shadow Falls.

ALI'S was by no means the first place of the sort into which Blake had penetrated that evening.

He had already visited three other haunts in various parts of the old city, and in each he had heard surreptitious whisperings of the affair that was the sensation of the underworld, as well as of the upper.

But not yet had he encountered any one of the half-dozen criminals whom he had dealt with on previous occasions, and with whom it might be safe to deal again. And he knew the terrific risk of making approach to any others.

He could, of course, have gone to Ripley Pasha, the Chief of Police, and from that official would have, received every courtesy for old friendship's sake. But he knew that Ripley Pasha was not free to give him carte blanche as formerly, and he was very chary of causing him any embarrassment.

The Zahmy Bey case would naturally come technically under the control of the Chief of Police; but Blake knew that the actual investigations would be in the hands of Egyptian inspectors and commandants.

It wasn't his aim to discover who killed Zahmy Bey, other than as that discovery might affect Mrs. Fortescue. It was her mysterious disappearance that was the puzzle he had decided to tackle, for, after further conversation with William Potter, and some cautious inquiries in certain quarters which shall be nameless, Blake had come to the conclusion that she really had left the palace.

One thing which neither he nor Potter knew was that the secretary was in possession of several facts which he hadn't passed on, not even to the native police inspector. And, through his position of authority in the household, he had seen to it that none of the servants did any babbling either.

Blake could not guess, therefore, that one of the women servants had been in league with Mrs. Fortescue up to the very moment of her going; nor that she had quailed then in terror of Zahmy Bey's wrath, and had fled to the innermost part of the harem.

Another item was her full confession to the secretary of the presence in the place of the recently engaged maid who had escaped with her mistress. But it wasn't she who told the secretary about the strange man who had been with Zahmy Bey when she burst in with the news that her mistress was taking flight. She could give a vague description of the man, but she had been in a state of collapse when he struck Zahmy Bey down, and could not swear that he had struck the blow. Nor had the other servants seen him clearly enough to add to her description.

But that secretary was no fool. He realised now that Zahmy Bey had been tricked. He guessed it was by some political enemy. And it didn't take much guessing to fix on the mysterious stranger as the one who had done the killing.

To find that man was his aim, and he knew he had much better chance of accomplishing his purpose without the aid of the police than with it. He was marking time, waiting for Zahmy Bey's brother to arrive from Assouan. Then they would get busy.

Hence there was little actual truth allowed to escape from the palace, and, in the underworld into which Blake had gone for news, it was sheer rumour and speculation, just as it was among the upper circles at the other end of the Muski and in the Boulevard Mohammed Ali.

Nevertheless, Blake believed that there was just a chance of picking up some hint among the haunts of the underworld. Zahmy Bey was a man of enormous interests, private, business, and political. His servants and other domestic dependants would number well over a hundred. His other affairs would bring another small army under his control. It was possible, Blake figured, that somewhere in that organisation there was a leak. If he could locate it —

But what he expected to find and what he came face to face with in Ali's were two very different things. It was not until he had penetrated to an inner room of the drinking shop where several forms of gambling were taking place that he received a considerable shock.

George Marsden Plummer!

Plummer was dressed almost as roughly as himself, and there were signs of a certain superficial disguise. But Sexton Blake had had too many dealings in the past with the master criminal to mistake his man.

He increased his own caution at once. Unless he came into direct encounter with Plummer there was little likelihood of the other recognising him. Yet he was taking no chances.

Not that he connected Plummer in any way with, the Zahmy Bey affair. There was nothing in what he had learned so far to cause him to suspect that Plummer might know anything about the killing. But he had learned from experience that where George Marsden Plummer might be there was good reason to keep a watchful eye.

It soon became obvious to him that Plummer had finished either the business or pleasure that had brought him to Ali's, for, slowly but surely, he was making his way towards the outer room.

Blake followed unobtrusively. It was when he was just passing through the curtained doorway and Plummer had already reached the middle of the front room, that Blake almost collided with a small rat of a fellow who turned a snarling, evil countenance up to him. But when he saw Blake's face his expression changed.

"The Greek!" he muttered. "I did not know —"

Blake drew him aside quickly.

"Quiet!" he warned him in a low, ugly tone. "You did not know I was in Cairo. Nor does anyone else. I have been looking for you. Come along."

"But I have —"

"Do you want me to cut your liver out?" interrupted Blake, with a snarl, "Come along!"

It was evident that, in the character of a crook known as "The Greek," Blake had caused considerable impression on his previous visits, for now the undersized rat of a fellow (who was a sneak-thief by profession) gave up whatever errand he had been bound on, and allowed Blake to haul him through the outer room. No one paid them any attention. That was a common enough sight in Ali's.

Plummer was just on the point of passing through the outer half-swing doors when Blake indicated him to his companion.

"Look at that fellow!" he muttered. "Look well!"

His companion did so, then turned an obliquely inquiring glance upon Blake.

"I want you to follow him," went on Blake. "I've got other business that will keep me here. You find out where he goes and come back here to tell me. Make sure he has gone to earth before you drop him. And if you fail —"

He pushed the other forward and stood watching until he, too, had passed through the doors into the alley beyond. He himself could have gone on Plummer's trail, but he knew that this gutter rat, who knew every twist and turning in the city, stood a much better chance of tailing Plummer undetected.

Himself, he lurched back into the inner room and stood up against a game of faro.

For two hours he stuck it, pressed in by unwashed crooks of every Eastern nationality. Since Plummer's departure he was the only European left, apart from Greeks.

But always his ears were attentive to every stray word that reached him; his eyes to the coming and going of everyone. He heard mention of the Zahmy Bey murder just as he had picked up bits in the other places he had visited. But nothing, not a whisper, that gave him any direct line, except that, several times, he heard the name, "Ferrand," or something like it. But that meant nothing —then.

At the end of two hours the rat whom he had sent to tail Plummer could be seen making his way through the gang in the outer room. Blake caught his eye and read an urgent signal. He left his stake on the table and pushed through to where the other stood.

"Come outside!"

He followed the other into the alley. They moved close to the wall that made a dead end, and, although they were perfectly visible as they stood, heads bent and close together, no one paid them any attention. Such private conferences were a common enough incident there.

"Well?" was Blake's curt demand.

"He got into a car as soon as he reached the Muski," was the whispered report. "It was not so easy then to follow him. But I managed. He did not drive so far along the Muski. He got out at a corner and the car drove away. I followed him on and saw him pause before a shop. He knocked there and was admitted. I waited for an hour until he came out. At first I did not know him. He was dressed as an effendi, in full dress and a shiny hat such as the cursed English put on at night."

"Ah! And then?"

"I saw the one of the shop. Then I remembered. He is not of Cairo. He comes from Paris. He wears a long beard, but it is not his own. He gives a good price for the stones if they are worth his trouble. He does not bother with small things. You know Paris? You would know him? His name is Ferrand."

"Never mind yet. I am interested in the other. Where did he go?"

"To the other end of the Muski. He entered the villa of an effendi.

He used a key. It must be his residence. I came back to tell you. Now, what does The Greek pay for this information? And, if he makes a play, do I receive a share?"

Blake pulled out some ragged bills and divided them.

"Here, take half of what I have. Now come with me."

JACQUES FERRAND was in a mood of combined fear and rage.

Fear, because the killing of Zahmy Bey was a thing he had never contemplated. Rage, because he had just had a most harassing interview with Plummer.

All too late, he told himself, he had learned what a fool he had been ever to have any transactions of any sort with Madame Zahmy Bey. And as for Plummer —well, the less thought about that the better.

Ever since the report had got abroad that Zahmy Bey had been murdered and Madame Zahmy Bey had disappeared he had been in a frenzy of terror lest, firstly, she should come to his shop, and, secondly, that there would be some evidence left behind at the palace which would connect him with the affair. In view of his reason for leaving Paris, he couldn't afford such a thing now, at any cost.

All that day he had lurked in the shadowy interior of the shop, starting affrightedly at every sound, peering furtively through the curtains at the back whenever the door opened. Hour after hour he had hoped, yet feared, that Plummer would come.

He hadn't the ghost of a notion what had happened, except that someone had killed Zahmy Bey, and the woman was blamed for it. There wasn't a whisper connecting Plummer or any other man with it. But Jacques Ferrand knew Cairo, and he knew its devious ways.

The day had drawn out, and the call of the muezzin to prayer had gone forth from a thousand minarets. Yet Plummer did not come. Had he succeeded in getting out of Cairo? Was he already out of Egypt? Had he himself been left to hold the baby?

He didn't put the question to himself in the English idiom, but that is what he meant.

Throughout the evening he sat in the back room without a light. In this way he could leave the curtains open a little so as to keep a surveillance on the front. He could see people passing back and forth, and every time someone paused before the shop his heart went into his mouth. It might be Plummer, or it might be the police. Either way he was afraid.

And then Plummer had come. It was an unpleasant interview. Plummer rode the high horse and demanded a large sum of ready money; Ferrand pleaded and begged for some guarantee of safety, if not of repayment or share.

The result was inevitable. Coolly Plummer had forced him to hand over a thousand pounds in cash, remarking easily as he pocketed it:

"That will do for the getaway, old-timer. I wouldn't have come to you, but I didn't anticipate this. I'm going to make a break when it is possible, but I may have to lie low for a bit. When we get out of the country, and Mrs. Fortescue can cash in on some of her own stuff — well, you will get your share, my friend. She thinks she is going to get off easy, but before she finishes she will know better. It is worth something to have her old man bumped off and be made a free widow. Don't you agree?"

And Ferrand had quavered:

"So it was you who did it? And now you leave me here —leave me behind. What of the police? What shall I do if they discover that she came to me? There are the servants who brought her in the ear? Did the waiting-woman escape, too?"

Plummer was not smiling.

"Listen, old-timer! I grant you that the position is not easy. That fool of a waiting-woman caved in at the last moment —lost nerve. What they'll get out of her at the palace, I don't know. Now that Zahmy Bey is dead and her mistress is gone, she may have sense enough to hold her tongue, or she may spill the lot."

"Heavens above me? And me, what shall I do?"

"If she holds her tongue you are all right. If she spills the beans, you'd better make a quick getaway. I'm making for Marseilles and Paris myself. You'd better do the same."

"You know I dare not put foot in France."

"Well, that's your candle to burn. But I'll let you know if I hear anything further. In the meantime, I've got my own hands full. I didn't want to bump off that bird, but I had to hit quick."

There was more wrangling and argument, but when Plummer took himself off, after changing his disguise in the back room, Ferrand was in a more perturbed state than ever.

And, considering the state of his nerves, it is little wonder that when, about an hour after Plummer's departure, there came a low, insistent tapping at the front door, he should have jumped half out of his chair, crept fearfully through the curtains, and gone tiptoeing along the shop.

Blake scrambled to the balcony. Shots from his automatic sent the gang in the courtyard back under cover.

HE could only make out two indistinct forms in the entry, one tall and one short.

He crept closer, his movements concealed by the inner gloom, until he was within a couple of feet of the glass panel. All the time the low, insistent knocking continued, and then suddenly Ferrand was startled into fresh terror as a blinding light struck him full in the face. It held him focused for no more than a couple of seconds. But that was enough to reveal him fully, and, as the flashlight was switched off, a low voice reached him.

"Open, Ferrand! Open at once. It is about Plummer, and no time to lose."

The fence stood frozen in his tracks. He knew it wasn't Plummer outside the door. Yet Plummer's name had been used. Nor could it be the police. They wouldn't approach in that fashion. Could it be someone from Zahmy Bey's household —someone seeking private vengeance?

He would have fled, had he dared. But where to go? There was a second way out all right. He had seen to that when he took the place. Few places in that part of Cairo didn't have a means of surreptitious ingress and exit.

But that low knocking had started again. Drawn by the power of his fear, Ferrand crept forward and turned the key. Instantly the door was pushed open. Two figures stepped into the shop. One of them gripped him by the arm and held him. The other closed the door and locked it.

Then the one who held him pushed him along the shop.

"Go ahead, Ferrand, and watch your step! Take us somewhere where we can talk safely. And no tricks."

The man spoke in French, spoke in tones of curt command which Ferrand did not know, but which he obeyed. He had no choice. He moved down the shop and through the curtains into the back recess. There he turned on a green shaded light, and, lifting fearful eyes, gazed at the man who held him.

But he recognised no one with whom he had had dealings. Yet when he turned his gaze, to the second intruder he recognised him quickly enough as a sneak-thief from whom he had bought a few trifles. He began to breathe easier. They had used Plummer's name, but this rat could have no connection with the Zahmy Bey affair. If it was just an ordinary hold-up he would know how to deal with it.

He stiffened under the grasp of the tall one, and strove to draw away. He began to bluster, but a twist of the arm cut him short.

"Enough, Ferrand!" the tall one snarled. "I thought there must be some mistake, for your disguise is excellent. I should have passed you in the street without a second glance. But now, what would our friend Emile Thibaud, of the Paris Surete, give to know that Jacques Ferrand was carrying on business as a fence in Cairo? There is still that ugly affair in Paris for which he is wanted."

Ferrand collapsed so that Blake had to heave him into a chair. This was something for which the curio dealer had not bargained. It came to him that Plummer, before making his getaway, had betrayed him to these two scoundrels. But then, as his brain cleared a little, he knew that could not be so. This fellow spoke in such easy French, he used the name of Thibaud— Emile Thibaud, the dreaded chief of the Brigade Mobile, in Paris. It must be a man from the Surete . . .

Blake saw well enough what was going on in the other's mind. His face betrayed his mental process as if it were a mirror. He gripped him even harder.

"Plummer has not betrayed you —yet, Ferrand," he said curtly. "But if you would save yourself it is up to you. What had he, and what had you to do with the Zahmy Bey affair? If you don't talk to me here I'm going to haul you along to Ripley Pasha, who will use other means."

"Who —who are you?" chattered Ferrand.

"Never mind! It is enough that I am looking for the American woman. I want to know where she is, and you are going to tell me. What part did you play? Did you kill Zahmy Bey as you killed that poor girl in Paris?"

Ferrand gave a squeak of terror.

"No, no, not" he gasped. "It was not I. It was . . . "

"Plummer?"

"No —I cannot speak. For the love of the saints, who are you? I know nothing; I have never seen the woman."

Blake bent his face close until his eyes bored into Ferrand's.

"No? Then why do they speak the name of Ferrand in Ali's place? Someone in the palace has talked, Ferrand, and if you would save yourself you had better talk, too —now."

Ferrand employed every resistance of which his devious mind was capably, but, slowly, ruthlessly, Blake dragged from him the story of his compact with Mrs. Fortescue and Plummer.

It was all clear enough to Blake now —he knew well what hand it was that had struck down Zahmy Bey. And he knew, too, that William Potter was right —his sister could not have done such a deed.

But she —where was she? Ferrand must know, and Ferrand must speak, no matter how he feared Plummer. For a few moments Blake debated whether he should reveal his identity to the fence; then he decided against it. He would continue to play his hand as it was.

Standing at one side was the gutter rat, growing more and more puzzled as matters proceeded. The other two were speaking in French, but the rat understood enough to gather something of what was going on. And as he absorbed a few words here, a few there, he began to tell himself that "The Greek" was behaving in a peculiar way for his kind. He did not seem to be making any attempt to rob the fence. He seemed only interested in the affair that had taken place at the Zahmy Bey palace. It didn't look as if there was going to be much in it for him.

His doubts came to an abrupt ending, as did Blake's questioning of Ferrand. All three were startled by a loud and furious hammering at the front door.

CURIOUSLY enough, it was Ferrand who found words first: "The police!" he gasped.

Blake jerked round, and jumped for the light switch. Then he caught hold of the rat.

"Go! Go quickly, and see what you can."

The rat slid through the curtains, and went along the shop like a soft-footed cat. Blake felt through the darkness, and grabbed Ferrand.

"No nonsense!" he warned. "How do we get out of here?"

There was no need to whisper. The hammering at the door made such a din. It seemed that only the police would dare to create such an uproar at that hour of the night, but Blake knew otherwise when the rat came back and said:

"Two big, closed cars in the street, half a dozen men at the door —not police. They'll be in in a moment."

"Zahmy Bey's men!" rasped Blake. "That woman has spilled the story. There they come. Up, Ferrand!"

Ferrand, now roused to the sense of his own imminent danger, came to his feet with a bound. There was a terrific crash in the front shop, and a spattering of broken glass. Now voices came to them clearly, and a light burst out, revealing through the parted curtains a mob of natives rushing along the shop.

Blake knew that only swift action could save them. If they were indeed Zahmy Bey's men, then they had learned the truth, and had come to tear the facts out of Ferrand.

Moreover, he knew perfectly well the embarrassment of his own position if he were caught and identified. It would mean that Ripley Pasha would be drawn into it, and, as he believed —if these were Zahmy Bey's men —that the intrusion was part of a private plan to investigate the murder and exact punishment without the interference of the police —that it might be part and parcel of a deeper plan to get hold of Mrs. Fortescue and get her back into the safety of the harem. Blake's unmasking would prove serious in more ways than one.

So when the rat came slithering through the curtains, and the gang rushed after him, Blake dragged out his pistol and shot three times, aiming low but taking good care that the bullets should thud into the planking just in front of the intruders.

The move was momentarily effective. The leaders skidded to a stop. They had not expected a reception of this sort from Ferrand. Blake took full advantage of it.

Wheeling, he grabbed Ferrand again, he hissed a single word in his ear:

"Out!"

Ferrand needed no further urging. He sprang across the recess and hauled at a curtain that hung against the wall. Blake and the rat were close on his heels.

The light in the front shop had been dowsed, but Blake knew from a sudden current of air on his cheek that Ferrand had got a panel open. He kept hold of Ferrand's coat so there should be no hanky-panky, and he could feel the rat squirming close to his own thighs.

Ferrand lurched forward through the opening, and Blake followed. The rat kept getting tangled in Blake's legs. Literally, they tumbled in a heap, down half a dozen steps, to find themselves in a narrow passage.

Blake scrambled to his feet, then flattened himself against the wall as someone above began shooting. When a bullet thudded into the wall close to his ear he considered himself justified in making reply. This time he did not shoot low.

Flinging up his weapon he aimed into the blinding heart of the light that was now at the top of the steps. On the crash of the shot it disappeared to the accompaniment of a shrill squeal of pain. Then he turned and pushed the other pair ahead.

"Quickly, quickly, Ferrand, if you would save yourself!"

The fence did not need the urging.

The shots had been sufficient. They went tumbling along the passage until they came to a second flight of steps that brought them again to the same level as the shop. A passage, then a door, and they were in a room which was lit by a single oil lamp.

On a couch, in filmy draperies, was a dark-skinned, dark-haired woman. On a stool close to her, with a stringed instrument on his knees, was a man, a swarthy-looking fellow.

The woman made as if to scream, but a fierce word from Ferrand stopped her. The man sprang to his feet. Ferrand motioned him away. He said something in what Blake knew to be Hebrew. Then with an upraising of the arms and a moan of terror, he ran towards a door.

What relation the pair were to Ferrand Blake couldn't guess. Nor did he care. The chief thing was that the old scoundrel seemed to know his way through the warren well enough. And, a moment later, as they rushed into a small courtyard, Blake knew that the chase was by no means over. From behind them came an uproar of harsh voices and screams.

In the centre of the courtyard was a fountain, not playing. Beyond that was a low, very narrow arch. More than that Blake could not see, for the fugitive light that filtered into the courtyard from some unseen source did not penetrate the gloom beyond the arch.

Whimpering, twisting his hands, Ferrand darted towards the black slit. But, the moment he started through, he drew back, emitting a yell of terror. Then Blake saw the reason. Just emerging from the gloom were two ruffianly-looking fellows, pistols drawn.

ONE of them shot deliberately at Ferrand. Only the fence's terror-stricken jumping saved him from death. Blake did not give the fellow a chance to shoot a second time. Flinging up his own weapon, he fired twice.

One man went down in a heap. The other whirled about and vanished in the darkness beyond the arch. But Blake knew it was hopeless to go that way. The leader of the gang, whether he came from the Zahmy Bey faction or not, knew the intricacies of the city.

He had figured on a secret means of exit and had provided against that risk.

Now, behind them, the clamour of the pursuers came louder. In a few moments they would be in the courtyard. Blake cast about him desperately. Just above him, on the right, was a low, rickety-looking balcony. There was no time to ask Ferrand whither it led.

Catching hold of the fence, he heaved him up, and sent him crashing through the rotten rails. There was no need to assist the rat. He was already going up like a monkey.

Blake caught hold of the edge and drew himself up. He rolled through the broken portion and scrambled to his feet. At this moment the gang began pouring into the courtyard, but a couple of shots from his automatic sent them back under cover for the moment.

The rat now began to display a sudden initiative. He evidently began to realise that, if he were caught by the mob at his heels, it would go harder with him than if he fell into the hands of the police. Or it may be that he recognised some of them and knew whence they came.

At any rate, he quite definitely decided to cast in his lot with "The Greek," and it was his foot that went smashing through the wooden shutter that covered the nearest window.

Blake followed him into a small, dirty room, that smelled of stale smoke, drink, and the unwashed. A repellent place it was, but, at the moment, its usual occupant was not at home.

Blake paused only long enough to haul Ferrand after him; then he dragged him across the room.

"Where is this? What house? Where does it bring us?"

"A low lodging place," chattered Ferrand. "It will have two ways, one to the front and one to the back."

"Then lead us to the front."

"But those men," began Ferrand.

"Shut your mouth. Do as I say!"

He dragged the rat aside and flung Ferrand into a gloomy hall that was lit by only a smoky oil lamp. He literally rushed Ferrand along until they came to a flight of stairs. Down these they tumbled, into another room, through that into still another passage, and then, almost before they realised it, they were in the street some three doors from Ferrand's shop.

There, Ferrand flinched and the rat cowered into a dark corner of the entry. Close to them was the foremost of the two big limousines in which the gang had come. But Blake did not give them a chance. He knew that, if he could reach the Muski not many yards away, he would be safe for the moment —if the attacking party did not belong to the police.

He pushed them on to the pavement and propelled them towards the Muski. At the same moment someone jumped down from the first car and shouted. Then, a gun crashed out, the bullet ricochetting from the pavement close to Blake's left foot.

He whirled round and pressed the trigger of his own weapon. The man who had leaped from the car went down. But second had already appeared.

Blake pressed the trigger again. This time there was no explosion. He had used his last cartridge. He turned then, and began to run. He carried the other two along with him and swung round into the Muski.

There, people were running towards them, attracted by the sound of the firing. Blake bent his head close to the rat's ear.

"You will know a den near here. Get us there —quick!"

They came into a walk, and two minutes later were diving down a dark flight of steps. Next, Blake found himself in a small, low-ceilinged hovel that was packed with a score of criminals of the rat's kidney.

It was, in a way, that crook's club.

Chapter 7. Getaway.

PLUMMER was in a dilemma.

He would have been the first to acknowledge that the killing of Zahmy Bey had been a great mistake. As a matter of fact, he hadn't intended hitting so hard. There had been no time to gauge the strength of the blow. Everything had rushed to a crisis so swiftly that each action had to be one of effective precision.

Nevertheless, when, early in the morning, he heard that Zahmy Bey was dead, he knew that he would have to scrap his original plan and think up something else.

As he and Vali Mata-Vali saw things they stood thus:

Their chief object had been accomplished —they had got Mrs. Fortescue out of Zahmy Bey's clutches.

On the other hand, Zahmy Bey had been killed. This, in the case of one so powerful as he, was bound to create terrific complications.

Next, the waiting-woman upon whom so much had depended, had thrown in her hand at the last moment through fear. There was a great risk in what she could tell; and, knowing something of the methods of the country in the dealings of an all-powerful master with his dependants, Plummer didn't think it would be long before she told all she knew. Of course, Zahmy Bey would not be the one to interrogate her, but there would be relatives and the secretary.

After that, there were the servants who had been brought on the scene by the screams of the other woman. They must have caught at least a fleeting view of him.

And, by no means least, there was Ferrand. If that waiting-woman told all she knew, then Ferrand would be a distinct danger. He must see Ferrand as soon as it was safe, and make certain that he was fixed properly. Moreover, he must manage somehow to get his charge out of the country. To that end, he must learn, if possible, just what steps were being taken regarding Zahmy Bey.

It wasn't only the complications created by the death of Zahmy Bey that made Plummer regret the force of his blow. The death of the Egyptian ended, once and for all, the chance of a double play which he had contemplated.

Once he had Mrs. Fortescue in his power he would have two strong lines to follow. If she should prove too difficult, then he could have put up a counter proposition to Zahmy Bey. In order to get his wife back into his hands Zahmy Bey might have been prepared to pay a far larger sum than the woman herself. And, once the deal was concluded, there would have been less risk for Plummer. But that possibility was ended now.

He was not worried very much about the fact that it was actually he who had finished off Zahmy Bey. Rumour had it that Madame Zahmy Bey was being accused of the deed, and Plummer realised that, in this, his hold over her was greatly strengthened. But he couldn't play that up until he got the real strength of what the underworld was saying.

Hence his visit to Ali's the evening following the killing. Like Blake, he prowled about other dives as well, and, unlike Blake, he managed to pick up many items of considerable interest. Plummer's contact with the criminal underworld of Cairo was more recent and active than Blake's.

What he did hear caused him to be more nervous than ever about Ferrand as a danger. Therefore, his visit to the fence. He did not care two straws what happened to Ferrand so long as he was not dragged into matters. And when he finally took leave of Ferrand he was satisfied that he had put greater fear into the fence than could be instilled by either police or any of Zahmy Bey's people. What had taken place in Paris was a stronger weapon than anything else. So he believed. Naturally, he knew nothing of the imminent visit of Sexton Blake, or of the raid which was to follow almost on Blake's heels.

On his return to the secluded villa at the upper end of the Muski, he took Vali Mata-Vali into the reception-room.

"How is she?" was his first question.

"Terrified."

"You told her that she is accused of the killing?"

"Yes, and piled it on thick."

"Well, we've got to make a getaway —quick!"

"Is there anything fresh?"

"No; but I can't trust Ferrand."

"How about money?"

"I've plenty. If we can get to Alexandria safely we can find a boat there."

"And then?"

"Along the North African coast as far as Morocco, then into the lower Riff country. We would be safe there, and could keep her in our hands until we cashed in."

"She may prove difficult."

Plummer grinned.

"I'll see that she is persuaded. Now take me to her."

MRS. FORTESCUE was lying on a couch in the large, luxuriously furnished bedroom which had been allocated to her. She was still wearing the clothes of a high-class Mohammedan woman, but was, of course, now unveiled.

Plummer, a swift reader of human emotions, saw at first glance that she was in a state of exhaustion through tension and fear. But there was no time to lose. He had made up his mind that they must leave Cairo this very night. So he went straight to the subject, though he was suave enough.

"I should like to have given you more time for rest," he said easily; "but, unfortunately, I believe it is best that we should get away within the hour. Mademoiselle has told you what is being rumoured?"

The American woman shivered. She had hated Zahmy Bey well enough. She had been terrified by him. And she had been prepared to pay a high price to escape. But she had never counted on killing. Such a thing had never touched her life before. And she was in a condition of cold terror at the thought that she was held to have done the deed.

"Is it true that I am accused of —"

She faltered.

"I am afraid so," finished Plummer gravely.

"But you —it was you who —"

"Who, unfortunately, struck harder than I intended. That is true, and all in good time I shall take pains that the truth is known. But it would do no good now. I might be apprehended if I went and confessed, but that would leave you and mademoiselle quite unprotected, and it is certain that the adherents of your late husband would leave no stone unturned to get you back in their powers.

She knew what he said was true. That was the weakness of her present position.

"What are you going to do?"

"It was my intention, as you know, to get you across the Mediterranean to France or some other country, where you would be safe. But now I must think of myself as well. I am still ready to carry out my promise, but the conditions must be —er —a little different. You realise that at any moment we may be discovered, and if I am to clear your name of that accusation I shall be placing myself in great jeopardy. Therefore I have a new proposal to make."

She sat up, arranging her disordered hair. She was really beautiful, Plummer decided, although there was little strength of character in her face.

"What is it?" she asked haltingly, glancing from him to Vali Mata-Vali and back again.

"You were prepared to pay well if I got you away?"

"Yes, oh, yes, and still am."

"No exact figure was discussed?"

"No; but I am still rich, and would not quibble about the price."

"Shall I tell you what I had intended asking?"

"Yes."

"One million dollars —two hundred thousand pounds."

"I would have paid it as soon as I got hold of some securities."

"The additional risk has altered things now. We cannot go direct to France. I must plunge into more expense and much more risk. I am still willing to do so if you will give me a written promise to pay me the figure I shall name."

"What is it?"

"Five million dollars."

"But that is preposterous! It is more than half the fortune I have left."

"Not quite half," returned Plummer smoothly. "But, even so, would you rather part with that and have still a large fortune left than to fall into the hands of your late husband's adherents and be treated as his murderess?"

She may not have had strength of character, but she was no fool. She knew what lay behind his words. She glanced at Vali Mata-Vali as if for signs of help, but saw none there. The adventuress was smoking a cigarette and smiling.

"That —that is a threat!" she managed at last.

"Not a threat; merely the statement of an alternative."

"Then I am helpless. I have no choice but to accept."

"And I shall see that you do not repudiate the promise," Plummer assured her.

Had she only known that her own brother was even then in Cairo, seeking her; had she even guessed that Sexton Blake, the shrewdest detective in Europe, was hot on the trail, she could have held out. But, poor, harassed woman, she could only realise that Zahmy Bey's creatures were seeking her. She could only anticipate with horror a return to that prison from which she would never, never again have a chance of escaping. So she could do nothing but yield to these demands. But now she knew this suave, bearded man for a crook, and she knew that Vali Mata-Vali was his accomplice.

From the moment of her acquiescence Plummer lost no time in making his preparations. Leaving Vali in charge of what could now only be described as their prisoner, he descended to the ground floor and rang for the criminal who was acting as butler. They held close confab together for some minutes. Then the crook chauffeur was brought in and given his instructions.

Twenty minutes later everything was ready. The car was at the back. Vali Mata-Vali was assisting Mrs. Fortescue down the stairs. Plummer, with a long coat concealing his evening clothes, stood in the hall, smiling confidently.

Then, just as Vali Mata-Vali and her charge turned the newel post and started towards the rear end of the hall, there came a sharp, imperative knocking at the front door.

"The game's up, Plummer!
You can't get away with this;
you must know that," said
Blake. "We've got you cold!"

Chapter 8.   Plummer Takes His Choice.

PLUMMER didn't fool himself that there was any friendly social visitor on the other side of that door.

He knew that the crisis he had anticipated, feared, and, as far as possible, provided for, had arrived.

He shot out one hand and switched off the light. Then he ran along the hall until he overtook Vali Mata-Vali and Mrs. Fortescue. There was no need to tell Vali what to do. She knew as well as he, and she could find her way to the yard at the back in the dark without the aid of a light.

They sped through the rooms that lay between them and the kitchen quarters. All the time they could hear the sound of the knocker reverberating through the house. Then a bell began to shrill, bell and knocker together making row enough to wake the dead.

There was something very urgent and very determined behind that double summons. It was a demand that would not brook delay. Plummer knew nothing of the presence of Sexton Blake in Cairo, but he wasn't so far wrong when he guessed that Ferrand had caved in and spilled the story. He figured it was either police or adherents of Zahmy Bey. He feared the latter far more than the former.

He cursed himself that he hadn't taken a chance and cleared out without going into the bazaar. He could have seen Ferrand and, after warning him and squeezing him for more money, cleared out. He had cut things too fine. Well, he'd show them yet! If it came to a clash, he'd give them something to remember. He wasn't going to lose that million pounds for the whole of Zahmy Bey's crew and the police put together. Not he!

They stumbled through the kitchen quarters and into a passage. Vali Mata-Vali had sized up the situation as quickly as Plummer. He could hear her using Zahmy Bey's name. That was the stuff! Scare the American stiff, and she wouldn't make any trouble.

In the yard both the Levantine and the Greek boy were waiting. The car stood in the shadow, the engine just ticking over. From the direction of the house came a crash as the front door went in. A few more minutes and their flight would be discovered.

Vali Mata-Vali and her charge bundled into the car. Plummer pushed the Greek after them. He himself took the wheel, with the Levantine beside him. Then he eased in the clutch, changed quickly

58

into second, and slid past third into top, smoothly.

It was a powerful car. He had seen to that. By the time he was round the corner of the house and heading for the front gates he was already approaching forty. He swerved just in time as he saw another car standing just inside the gates. He had not yet switched on his lights, and was almost on top of the other vehicle before he saw it. But he missed it, and then, as someone sprang down and started to run towards the house, Plummer swung the big limousine into the Muski, and at the same moment switched on the lights.

As the speedometer needle crawled from forty to fifty, and from fifty to sixty, Plummer had time to think of what he had just seen.

One car only. No men in uniform. It wasn't the police who had broken into the house. It could only be Zahmy Bey's men. He grinned at the thought. He felt safer now. With this powerful monster leaping beneath his touch, answering every move of finger and foot, he felt as if he were riding on top of the world. And in the back was a million pounds! Alexandria —he'd make it in under four hours. Let them tear the villa to pieces for all he cared. Let them overtake him if they could.

AS a matter of fact, it took Sexton Blake less time than Plummer reckoned to realise that he had arrived just too late. He was in the dining-room of the villa when he heard a car pass the side of the house. He guessed what was happening. He had already reached the hall, when the rat came plunging through the doorway to tell him that a car had dashed through the gate, and was racing down the Muski.

Blake gave an exclamation of chagrin. If he had not stopped to pick up William Potter on his way, he would have been in time. Potter was gazing at him in perplexity. He didn't understand what it all meant. Ferrand, too much in fear of Plummer to enter the house, was still in the car which Potter had secured instead of the taxi in which Blake had driven to Shepheard's.

"Come on!" was all Blake said.

But at the wheel of the car, with Potter beside him, he was more informative.

"We've got to pick up the trail before they get clear of Cairo. He will make for either Port Said or Alexandria. He daren't go south,"

Blake knew that, which ever road the fugitives should take — whether to Port Said or Alexandria —they would almost certainly pass through Bulak, the port and suburb of Cairo.

There was no hope of picking them up along the Muski, or in the Boulevard Mohammed Ali. Plummer had had too much start for that.

It was the rat, as a matter of fact, who now came in useful. That individual didn't know yet that he was, for the first time in his life, working on the side of law and order. He still be believed that "The Greek" was out to muscle in on another crook's game, and he looked upon Potter, with his American twang, as some sort of flash gunman.

In Bulak, among the streets of which he had prowled many a time, and where he knew every other crook, he slid out of the car and disappeared. But he was back within a few minutes with the information that Blake wanted.

This was to the effect that a big, closed car had gone through at high speed less than ten minutes before, and, as far as could be judged, was headed towards Tanta.

"If that is so, then it is making for Alexandria," Blake told Potter. "If they were trying for Port Said they would have taken the road to Zagazig. We'll try Tanta."

On they sped once more, leaving Bulak behind, tearing past groups of huts that grew less and less frequent as the miles were left behind.

At Tanta they stopped again. It was necessary, in any event, to fill up with petrol, and at the station Blake ascertained that a car such as he described had also refuelled there just before he drove up.

Three or four minutes. Plummer was still driving hard, but evidently not so terrifically as he had begun. Blake himself had been clocking close to sixty ever since leaving Bulak, and now, as he got clear of Tanta, he settled down behind the wheel, and gave her all she could take.

Forty, forty-five, fifty, fifty-five, sixty, sixty-three. He held her there, for in places the sandy road was bumpy with little drifts of sand, and he knew how perilous they could be if he started to skid.

Between Tanta and Alexandria were only a few small villages and hamlets, through which he would roar at un-diminished speed. All the time, both he and Potter were staring ahead, along the tunnels of light cast by the powerful road lamps, ready for the first sign of the other car.

It was certain that Plummer would spot those brilliant lights before they could discern him. That meant that Plummer would have his engine all out. Then it must become a matter of which possessed the most speed.

At least, this was Blake's theory. But the actual denouement was different. It was Potter who first spied something at the side of the road far ahead. He touched Blake's arm. Blake saw the object and nodded.

"It may be our quarry," he conceded. "Perhaps a puncture or engine breakdown. I'm going to slow down. If that is Plummer he may open up with a gun."

He was not mistaken. When he was still some fifty yards from the other car, and was drawing in to stop at the side of the road, he saw a man run round to the back of the car ahead, and then next moment a bullet plomped against the glass windscreen.

It did not smash the glass, but ricochetted off into the sand.

"Distance too great," said Blake laconically "This is going to be difficult, Potter. We can't risk hitting your sister. And if Plummer guesses our identity, he'll make plenty of play on that. I want you to remain here —you and the others. I'll slide out and work round to the back of the car. Then I'm going to get off the road. I may be able to work my way round in the dark. If I can catch him on one side I'll get the drop on him."

He did not give the other time to protest. Getting out, he kept close to the side of the car, paused to speak a word to the rat and the terrified Ferrand though the open window, then he dived into the velvety darkness.

Plummer was still shooting. The bullets were pattering against the car and into the sand. But he was doing no real damage yet. Blake ignored the shots. He wanted to get closer, to catch Plummer at an angle where he could not use his own car or Mrs. Fortescue as a defence.

But when he had covered less than a dozen yards, he saw Plummer turn back round to his car and disappear. Blake began to run. He was within a score of yards of his objective when it began to move. The breakdown, whatever it was, had been repaired, and now he could only stand for the moment and fume as he watched the big limousine go lurching along at ever increasing speed.

HE turned and made at top speed for the road. Then, risky though it was, he began to shoot, aiming at the low rear of the disappearing vehicle.

The result was confusing and amazing. The moving area of light in front of the speeding car seemed to swing round slowly in a semicircle, until it lit up the barren sand to the east of the road.

Then it wavered back and forth in agitated fashion before coming still.

Blake knew well enough what had happened. One or more of his shots had been lucky. One or more tyres had been hit. It had needed all Plummer's adroitness to keep the car from turning over. And now it was stalled, sidewise on the road.

Blake turned towards the car behind and made urgent gestures with upraised arms. He was standing bathed in the bright light from that vehicle, and almost at once he felt the increasing intensity of the twin headlights as they approached.

He jumped on to the running-board while the car was still moving.

"Keep on, keep on!" he ordered Potter, who was at the wheel. "Drive straight up to him!"

With his automatic clutched in his right hand, and clinging on with his left, he held himself ready to meet any attack that Plummer might launch. But none came. When only a dozen yards separated the two vehicles, he motioned to Potter to stop.

Himself, he leaped on to the road and began to run forward. A weapon spat then, and a bullet whizzed past his ear, though he could not see the person who had fired it.

He drew up then, a full fair target, but his hands were in the air. He dared not shoot now for fear of hitting Mrs. Fortescue. And he knew that, even in the brilliant light, Plummer would not recognise him in that get-up. He knew his only chance now was to make a bold play. If that failed, Plummer had him at his mercy. If it proved effective, then bloodshed would be prevented. He had to think first of the safety of the woman.

"Better put that gun away and talk, Plummer," he called, his voice carrying easily on the still night air. "Come out from cover and talk. I think you will know who is speaking!"

And Plummer knew.

Sexton Blake!

How Blake happened to be there at that moment he couldn't guess. But that it was Blake and not the police or any of Zahmy Bey's crew, was plain. And he knew, too, that he had no choice, for he could not proceed in his own car until the riddled tyres had been changed.

He stepped into view and advanced. Closer and closer he drew to Blake, until they were but a yard apart.

"The game's up, Plummer," he said quietly. "You can't get far with this. You must know that Zahmy Bey's people are combing the city for you. They'll soon be this far and —beyond. Then the police. You know as well as I do that the accusation against Mrs. Fortescue won't hold water for a moment once a real investigation is started. This is her brother. We've got you cold! I don't know what your game is, but you've got to drop it! We want Mrs. Fortescue, and we are going to have her! In return, I'll hand over a friend of yours — Ferrand. Are you going to listen to reason or . . . ."

Plummer was silent. It was plain that he was weighing his chances. He might kill Blake. He could probably kill Potter, but that would be a fatal move so far as his dealings with Mrs. Fortescue were concerned. And Zahmy Bey's crowd. He knew Blake wasn't bluffing there. But that million . . .

"I'll see Mrs. Fortescue," he began, but Blake cut him short,

"No! We settle this here and now. You have been playing for a big stake, and I know that Mrs. Fortescue would not get out of your hands until she paid a high figure. Well, you're not going to get it, Plummer, I dare say you have already received something from her. You can keep that, but no more. Mrs. Fortescue comes with us. Ferrand goes with you. You can have it which way you like.

"Personally, I think you would be a fool to continue on to Alexandria! And you would be putting your head in the noose to return to Cairo. If I were you I should go west. You can make El Hamman from here, and get camels. Then you can follow the caravan trail to Siwa. From there it is only a jump into Tripoli —Italian territory. I'd get out of Egypt as quickly as possible if I were you. That's all! What is it to be?"

Plummer looked up into the starlit sky. He gazed through the purple blanket of night that lay over the Libyan desert. Then he twisted round and gave one glance at the disabled motor-car. He was grinning when he faced Blake again.

"You win!" he said laconically. But Blake knew nothing of the diamonds which Plummer had tucked away safely. He only learned of that when, some two hours later, they were back in Cairo.

Only then did he approach Ripley Pasha regarding the killing of Zahmy Bey. What he was able to tell the Chief of Police about

Plummer and Mrs. Fortescue's statement, which he had laid on the other's desk, were sufficient to clear her of the monstrous charge.

But that harassed woman was in a state of nervous anxiety until, two days later, she and her brother with Blake were on board a P. & O. boat headed for Marseilles.

And, as they left the point of Damietta behind, Blake looked towards the flat coast. He was wondering how the little caravan was faring, that must, even then, be plodding along on its way to Siwa.

Plummer —Vali Mata-Vali —Jacques Ferrand! What would be the outcome, with those three alone in the desert bound together by their knowledge of each other's crimes?

But that, as Blake remarked to Potter, was not their funeral.

THE END
[22700 WORDS]

The thrill of a slow suspense climbing to an inexorable climax; a strange insight into the devious twistings of the criminal mind; the power and grip of a story fascinatingly told . . . . that's going to be your—

By Phyllis Drew

Between him and a millionaire's money were three lives, and so • • • •

FIRST INSTALMENT of a brilliant, powerfully written *short* serial of insight and human appeal.

Begin NOW this dramatic story of a doctor's crime.

—*impression of this enthralling Phyllis Lewis story, which surpasses even the last serial of hers which we published,* "*Chains of Fate,*" *and which will perhaps be even more acclaimed than was that very popular serial.*

Chapter 1. *The Fortune Hunter.*

SUSAN CARSTAIRS' clinging, swaying body would have told Dr. Billy North that he had aroused ecstasy and rapture within her, even if her eyes had not telegraphed again and again the message, "I love you!"

Her rapid heartbeats whispered it, too, as he clasped her close, undulating to the negro orchestra's jazz, the music that was a half-savage cry of mate to mate, a primeval jungle call, to which, in his arms, her madly throbbing nerves responded.

The fashionable throng on the floor grew dim in her sight. She was lost in a delirium of emotion, so that she no longer saw the brightly coloured velvets and satins and diamonds that were women, the black-and-white figures that were men. She might have been alone with Billy North on a tropic desert island.

North, too, was vibrant and tense, dazzled by the glitter of the scene, intoxicated with the sense of his own power over the beautiful daughter of millionaire Carstairs. A hectic excitement seemed to flash back and forth between him and the girl so ardently gazing into his blue eyes, swift electric currents that quivered and tingled to the core of their beings.

With unexpected suddenness, the music stopped. People were moving toward the supper-room. The sound of champagne corks being drawn, the laughter and chatter of three hundred voices, recalled to them that, after all, they were not two elemental beings belonging to one another in a world of their own, but hostess and guest at a fashionable ball.

"Isn't it amazing that until to-night we were strangers, and now —"

Dr. North stopped short. He was watching Susan closely. Her alluring face was flushed, giving added vivacity to her large dark eyes. Her lips were parted, as she smiled to herself, a quaint, funny little smile, the smile of a child that knows it is about to have a. delicious surprise. She looked up at him.

"You were saying?" she encouraged.

Billy North hesitated to reply only for a brief instant. In that moment he had reviewed the situation —measured and weighed all that he stood to gain, and all that, through the slightest blunder, he might possibly lose. But his knowledge of human nature guided him. If he were to win the daughter of the famous millionaire, the girl whose normal destiny would be to marry riches and a title, his capture of her heart must be swift.

"I was telling you my thoughts —speaking aloud to myself, as it were," he said, "and I was thinking that it was an amazing thing that until tonight we had never know one another, and that now I am in love with you!"

His gaze never left her face. He was watching for the tiniest change of expression, the very slightest indication that would tell him whether to continue or to change his method of approach. But he had struck the right note.

Susan was not reflecting upon the fact that she was a millionaire's daughter. She was revelling in the knowledge that this handsome stranger —no, surely he was a stranger no longer —had fallen in love with her. The reckless excitement that had possessed her as she danced with him surged over her once again. He saw the sparkle of her eyes, and knew its significance.

"If you will finish your caviar and have just half a glass more champagne," he said, "you might show me your mother's rose-garden by moonlight. I understand that the lake there is very beautiful —and" —his voice sank— "very lonely."

Then his mood changed. Gone was the serious lover, and in his place was a mere boy, who cried gleefully, "I certainly think that we ought to go and cheer up a lonely rose-garden, don't you?"

Entering into his mood, she replied that she regarded it as an urgent duty.

Together they wandered into Mrs. Carstairs' rose-garden, strolling slowly toward the water-lily pool that was one of the beauties of the Carstairs estate. The moonlight cast on the water a sheet of pearl. With sudden ardour, North took Susan in his arms and kissed her. The scene was ideal for lovers. North silently thanked his stars for the perfume of roses, the romantic moon, and the moonlit waters of the lily pool, the shadows that made the world remote.

The moon's rays fell upon Susan's shimmering dress. She appeared as though she had been caught in a storm, and the raindrops had turned to diamonds.

Billy North told her so.

"I think that this evening's ball has been like the marvellous, things that you read of in fairy stories, and you —well, you are like the fairy princess!"

"How do you know that I am not a witch disguised?" she asked.

"I don't know, really, but then, you see, that doesn't matter. So long as you are you, I don't mind whether you are fairy or witch. I would love you anyway!"

They sat on the little garden seat close to the edge of the water-lily pool, and once again North, realising the storm of emotion that his caresses could arouse within her, drew her close to him and kissed her. But his keen eyes were watchful of every change of expression, every shade of feeling that reflected itself on that lovely young face.

When she had readied a state of half-dazed bliss he drew away from her suddenly. He spoke with a harshness that startled her.

"I can't let myself kiss you any more, Susan," he said. "Do you realise that we can't marry? To you and your people I should appear a pauper. I am a doctor, a scientist. I've never even tried to amass money. I make in a year a sum that your father would look upon as a pittance."

Susan's heart, which had missed a beat at his first words, now began to pound. She spoke softly, but with conviction.

"You don't know my father," she said. "Dad is not like that. He would rather that I married the man I loved than choose somebody because he happened to be rich."

"Your father might think I was a fortune-hunter." He said curtly. But his eager expression, calculatingly concealed by shadows, was strangely at variance with his words.

Susan responded as he had expected.

"My father is a good judge of character," she said, with dignity. "And I think that he can be relied upon to judge fairly. He likes you and respects you. That is why you were invited this evening. I think that he would be delighted if I married a man that he admired, and he would not care at all about money."

This was music to Billy North's ears. He knew that he had made a favourable impression upon the millionaire, but he wanted to hear it confirmed. It had been, in effect, Mr. Carstairs himself who had requested that an invitation be sent to Dr. North —hence his presence at the ball that night.

SOME days earlier Billy North had sought the advice of Mr. Carstairs, who owed his fortune to his expert knowledge of chemistry. He had wished to consult the old gentleman upon a technical point.

The two had got along so well together, the millionaire had been so taken by the delightful young physician, that he had asked him one or two personal questions. Thus, Billy had told him that he was a Canadian, and that he was practising medicine in London. He liked England, he said, and he enjoyed his work, but he was rather lonesome. Naturally, since he had arrived only a few months ago and had been working hard ever since, he had not had time to make many friends.

"I left Canada when my parents were killed in an accident," he had explained sadly. "I felt that the farther away I got the better. I was entirely alone in the world, and so I thought that I would take a chance and see what I could do in London. There would be nothing over here to remind me of all I had lost."

Mr. Carstairs himself felt that family affection was a beautiful thing, and his fatherly kindness had prompted him to say: "You mustn't go about imagining that you've got no friends in England. I'd like you to feel that you've got me, my boy."

With a schoolboyish gesture, Dr. North had seized the old gentleman's hand and wrung it.

"Gosh!" he murmured. "I can just picture my dad saying that."

The young physician's response had been so spontaneous, so natural, that Mr. Carstairs, thinking of his own son, Susan's twin, had suddenly become conscious of a tightness in his throat.

"I'd like you to meet my family, Dr. North," he said. "How about coming to a dance that I'm giving to celebrate the birthday of my youngsters —Susan and Harold, twins —nineteen years old?"

"Oh, I'd love it, sir," Billy answered, with all the eagerness of a boy.

It was this quality of youthful sincerity, coupled with the brilliant intelligence that Mr. Carstairs had not been slow to discover daring his technical discussion with North, that made the Canadian attractive in his eyes. Ever quick to judge men, he had come to the conclusion during that first meeting that North, although unworldly, was a scientist of promise. True, he would probably never develop the money sense, and never be "worth anything" from a financial point of view, but Mr. Carstairs, besides being a millionaire, was a man of intellect, and he was respectful of a masterly mind.

Instinctively his thoughts roamed toward Susan. She was so much like him that he could well imagine her falling in love with North. Ah, well, if it happened, he would not be the person to object.

Susan had money enough of her own. She had no need to link her fortune with a greater one. Better to marry the right sort of man, he reflected, than to worry about how much he had got.

Mr. Carstairs had a very sane notion as to the value of money. He neither overestimated nor underestimated it. He had a dread of fortune-hunters, as every millionaire must have, but he appreciated the difference between the man who was incapable of making his way and therefore must needs marry a rich girl, and the man who did not possess wealth because he chose to devote himself to work that he considered more important than moneymaking.

He said nothing of North to Susan, save to ask her to send him an invitation to the ball. He determined to let things take their course.

But when, simultaneously, he missed Susan and his young guest from the supper-room, he drew his own conclusions, smiled wisely into his beard, and told everyone who inquired for her that she had gone to fetch her mother a scarf. Earlier in the evening he had spent some time with North, and the more he saw of him the better he liked him.

He had observed, with approval, the joyous look upon Susan's fresh and lovely face when she had danced with the doctor, and although he had not guessed at the tumult of fiery emotion that raged within her, he had understood that she, too, had responded to the magnetic quality of the doctor's personality.

And he had been pleased. It always pleased him to see himself reflected in his daughter. It flattered his vanity to realise that there was a likeness between him and the exquisite, jewel-like being whose shining beauty drew every eye.

Eventually, however, Susan's absence began to attract attention, and the old gentleman asked his son, Harold, to look for her. He had a shrewd idea that she would wander with North toward that most romantic of spots, the water-lily pond.

Susan heard Harold's approaching footsteps, and thus he interrupted no love scene, but merely came upon his sister sitting decorously on the garden seat. In the rush and excitement of the evening he and the doctor had not met, and Susan introduced them.

Her nerves were so taut as to be sensitive to the slightest change in the atmosphere, and, to her distress, it came to her even as they shook hands and murmured conventional greetings that Harold and the doctor had failed to take that instantaneous liking to one another for which she had hoped.

Susan and her brother had always been close, bound by the peculiarly subtle sympathy that seems often to belong to two souls born together. And she wanted, she wanted very urgently, that Harold should like Dr. North, for she knew even then that she was going to marry him.

But Harold didn't like him. The slight stiffness with which he addressed North as he explained that Mr. Carstairs thought that it was getting chilly for Susan to be out in her evening things was sufficient to tell her that. North himself, however, appeared not to notice any constraint in the young fellow's manner. In his charming way he apologised for having detained Susan and the three strolled toward the house.

"Go back on me!" she exclaimed. "Did you really think I would let you do that . . . . that I would stand for that?"

Antipathy.

THE days that followed were wrapped in a golden haze of happiness for Susan. After displaying some hesitancy at the idea of marrying a girl possessed of so much wealth he had approached her father.

Never had Mr. Carstairs been more conscious of North's charm than when the young doctor explained that he adored Susan, but that his income was no more than a thousand a year.

"Awkward, isn't it, sir?" he had said, more as though Mr. Carstairs were his own father than Susan's, and he was seeking his advice and consolation. "One can't very well ask a girl who has been brought up in an atmosphere of millions to marry one if one has so small an income, can one? And yet we love each other."

"What does Susan say about it all?" inquired Mr. Carstairs, a twinkle in his eye.

"Susan says she doesn't care about the money, but, of course, I have to think of her future. She doesn't know what it means to have less than she's been brought up to. And the trouble is that I can't promise that I shall ever make any more."

The young man paused, and then went on:

"You see I am not really going to devote myself to making money. I want to pursue the scientific side of my work. If I did not stick to that I should go all to pieces, because it means so much more to me than money."

He was talking to a sympathetic audience. He felt the old gentleman's respect for him rising, as he continued:

"My position is pretty tough, sir, as you'll see, because if I don't marry Susan, success, even in my scientific work, won't count for much with me."

It was Mr. Carstairs' turn to speak. He considered that North had approached a delicate situation in a manly and altogether admirable way, and he was eager to help him.

"My boy," he said affectionately, "don't make the mistake of thinking that because I happen to be a successful man I am unable to appreciate that there are things in life that are more important than making money. I consider that your work is more vital than any fortune that you might possess. I shall take care of Susan and make things easy for you."

North's eyes lighted up.

"You are a real sportsman, sir, if I may say so," he blurted out boyishly. And then, as though at a loss for words: "I can't thank you, sir —can't think of how to put it. But you understand. And now, may I dash off to tell Susan?"

He had gone like a streak of lightning!

The old gentleman chuckled. The impetuousness with which North had rushed to tell Susan the good news, his unworldliness in not wishing to know the amount that his future father-in-law proposed to settle on him, had pleased the millionaire.

"He doesn't know whether I'm thinking in tens or in thousands," he murmured to himself. "Doesn't know, and doesn't care, so long as he can have Susan. Ah, well, I would not have it otherwise. I think the world of the boy. A magnificent brain —magnificent!"

But, highly as he esteemed Dr. North, Mr. Carstairs did him an injustice. He was a very much cleverer man than even the shrewd man of millions could suppose.

A little later, the doctor's want of commercial knowledge again afforded him amusement. He had made an appointment with his own solicitor, who was to attend to the marriage settlements, and he asked North for the name of his lawyer.

"I've never had a lawyer," said North, with the simplicity that always pleased Carstairs. "You see, I've never sued anybody, or been sued by anyone, and so I haven't needed one."

The idea of a human being minus a lawyer to take care of his interests so diverted the millionaire, who kept a large firm busy attending to his firm's commercial contracts, that he laughed loud and long.

"What about the settlements?" he inquired. "Don't you think that you ought to be represented?"

"Oh, you can represent me, sir," said North easily. "It's all right that way, isn't it?"

Still not a single question had he put as to what the old gentleman might be planning. Mr. Carstairs was so touched by this evidence of North's love for his bride-to-be that he vowed silently that he would be even more generous than he had previously intended.

The one cloud upon Susan's happiness was her twin's dislike of her fiance. Harold's queer antagonism, shown the very first time that he and the doctor had met, persisted. If Susan were puzzled about it, she was not more so than Harold himself. The effect that North produced on Harold was inexplicable.

The boy had no idea why he should feel, when Billy shook hands with him, as though a snake were coiling itself round him. He had not the dimmest notion as to why the very sight of him should cause repulsion to arise within him.

It was unjust —in fact, almost cruel —and Harold detested himself for a prejudice which, he assured himself over and over again, was absurd. But it was not within his power to alter it. It was just one of those unfortunate facts that must be reckoned with, and that no amount of effort will change.

More than once, Susan tried to discover the root of Harold's antipathy to the man she adored. He would answer questions feebly, with "Yes, of course, I know he's a fine chap," and "No, he has never been disagreeable to me," or words to that effect, but these efforts to explain away a state of feeling were worse than useless, for they distressed sister and brother alike.

AS the wedding drew near it became necessary for Susan to leave the country house, where North visited her at week-ends, and go to London, to order her trousseau and her wedding-dress.

Although she loved Carstairs House, with its flower-filled gardens, its water-lily pool, and its large park, she was not sorry, for she hoped thus to see more of her fiance. With her mother, she went to town, but when she began to visit the dressmakers, the milliners, and the endless people that seem to be in evidence only when a wedding is in the offing, she found that she had very little leisure, and that she spent only a little more time with Billy than when she was at home in Cheshire.

True, on the evenings that he was not working in his laboratory, they would go out together, sometimes in her racing car, which she would drive herself; that he might rest, and sometimes to one of the gay night clubs, which, as she was so young, were a stimulating novelty to her.

The brightness of the scene, the bevy of lovely girls in pretty frocks, the elegance of the young men, the music, the gold-necked bottles of champagne and the delicate foods, would recall to her vividly her first meeting with North, and she needed only to be reminded of that to feel that she was in heaven.

Each time that they would dance together, regardless of the presence of strangers, they would recapture the thrill of that night, and Susan would be stirred afresh.

But in spite of these happy interludes she longed to be with him more, and was delighted to find one day that she had managed to finish her fittings at an hour that coincided with the time at which his consulting hours were supposed to be over.

She drove to his surgery and suggested that she should motor him to some country inn for tea. He fell in with her plan with his usual boyish enthusiasm. But just as they had reached the hall, and were about to go, a disturbing incident occurred.

The bell had rung and the maid had opened the door.

Susan and Billy heard her say to the visitor, "The doctor's consulting hours are over, miss; you are just too late," when the maid was pushed unceremoniously to one side, and a girl burst in.

She was a striking-looking, red-headed girl, the very antithesis of Susan, who was a blonde, with hair of pure gold that contrasted attractively with her black eyes.

The visitor's gaze met that of the doctor, and for a moment she paused and looked him up and down, as though she were seeing for the first time that splendid figure, tall, broad of shoulder and narrow of hip, that carven face crowned with the thick, fair hair of the Norsemen of ancient lore, and which was saved from hardness only by the gentle expression of the deep blue eyes, the boyish candour of the smile.

Then her rage flared, and she spoke. "Go back on me, would you?" she said tigerishly. "Did you really think that I would let you do that? Did you kid yourself that I was the sort that would stand for that?"

The girl's eyes were snapping with temper, but it was not difficult to see that beneath her anger lay fear. Also the quaver of her angry voice indicated that she was not far from tears.

"Let's go back into my consulting-room," suggested the doctor calmly. "Come along as well, Susan. Since you have heard this young lady begin the recital of her troubles, perhaps you had better hear the end."

The two girls looked at one another questioningly as North ushered them into his surgery, and gave them seats. Suddenly the red-haired girl dissolved into a storm of weeping, unconsciously seizing Susan's hand and pressing it to emphasise her points.

"He's given me up!" she sobbed incoherently. "He won't have anything more to do with me. Night after night I've been expecting him to come to me. And not a word has he sent me —not even rung me up!"

Her sobs interrupted her narrative. Susan, white-faced and quivering, looked at the doctor, who had strolled behind the weeping visitor. He made a sign to her to be silent, and, although mystified and frightened, she obeyed. Then he came round to the front of the weeping girl and, placing his hands on her shoulders, gave her a sharp shake.

"Come, come!" he said sternly. "Is this the way to make me return to you?"

Dealing with Doll Fuller.

AT these words Susan's face became still paler. But she remained quiet. The doctor then placed his hand under the visitor's chin, and he raised her face until she looked straight into his eyes.

"You are to do as I tell you," he said authoritatively. "Do you understand? Exactly as I tell you?"

For a long moment all was silent, although the atmosphere grew tense with the force of the mental battle that was being fought between the man and the girl. At last the girl became submissive, almost as though he were putting some physical compulsion upon her.

"Y-yes," she said doubtfully; "I am to do exactly as you tell me. What do you want me to do?"

"I want you to go straight home and rest. Wait for me until I come. You are not to telephone to me or to send for me. You are not to bother me in any way. You are to leave everything in my hands."

As he spoke his eyes held the gaze of the red-haired girl, who now seemed utterly limp. She repeated in a monotone his instructions, and, having finished, began once more to say these aloud to herself.

Only when he removed his eyes did she pluck up a little spirit, and ask once again, with a ghostly echo of the passion that she had displayed at the beginning of the interview:

"You won't give me up? You promise?"

And once more he had looked right into her eyes and had said, evenly, but with a finality that was definite:

"I shall do just whatever I think best. Understand that, once and for all, and you will save yourself a good deal of trouble. However, I shall certainly come to see you and arrange matters. You may depend upon that."

The girl seemed to breathe once more. "You will come?" she murmured; and he nodded.

To Susan it was like watching the return to life of one who had lost consciousness. But her own heart was almost bursting.

Who was this girl? What claim had she on Billy? If she should lose Billy? She knew in that moment of suspense that if she lost Billy she would lose the world.

Meanwhile, the doctor, calm as ever, had rung the bell. The maid appeared.

"Show this young lady out," he said, and then shook hands with the red-haired girl, and bustled her out before she could follow up her obvious intention of speaking to Susan. He was as amiable as though the little scene of a moment ago had never taken place. "Good-afternoon!" he said to her. "Mind you do what I have told you!"

So soon as the visitor had departed he turned to Susan, whose eyes, however, were bright with unshed tears. He managed to convey to her the fact that he was surprised, as he came and knelt beside her and put his arms round her tenderly.

He was thinking fast, desperately fast, but his strenuous mental efforts did not reflect themselves upon his face, in which Susan read only concern for herself.

"You don't love her? Tell me you don't love her!" she implored.

The laugh that shook North sounded as spontaneous as that of a schoolboy who had played a trick on his headmaster.

"Love Doll Fuller," he cried— "love her? Susan, my precious, have you lost all your good sense, or only your sense of humour?"

But Susan saw nothing amusing in the situation. She did not smile.

"Tell me!" she begged. "I can't endure this uncertainty. Why did she speak to you like that? How dared she unless you were her —her sweetheart?"

"Of course I'll explain, dear," he said gently. "I forgot that you wouldn't understand. Poor Doll can't help behaving in that way. She is m.d."

"M.d.? I'm afraid that I don't know what m.d. means," murmured Susan slowly.

"Oh, I'm sorry!" cried the doctor. "Of course you don't. It means mentally deficient." His manner had become light. "Some call it 'bats in the belfry,' others 'nutty,' and still others express it in the one elegant word 'dotty'; but it all means the same thing —mentally deficient."

DO you mean to say that Miss Fuller is mad?" she asked, incredulous, and simultaneously relieved and horrified.

"That is a very interesting point," he said, dropping, as it were, unconsciously into his professional manner. "You see, the border line between sanity and insanity is difficult to define. I should say that she is not certifiable On the other hand, she is most certainly irresponsible, and" —he paused— "this is the most serious symptom she has shown. She suffers from delusions."

Her thankfulness was so great that Susan, although sincerely sorry for the unfortunate Miss Fuller, began to smile.

"Tell me more about her," she said. "Tell me what she meant by the things she said."

"It has been one of her recent delusions that I was going to marry her," he said, in the same professional and detached tone; "and her reproaches were due to the fact that I have not been to see her lately."

"She believed that you were going to marry her?" cried Susan, aghast once more. "But did you do anything to make her believe such a thing? It seems so extraordinary!"

"Oh, no, not extraordinary! The delusion that men are in love with them is quite common among hysterical women patients," he replied. "I believe, as a matter of fact, that she thought that the doctor who attended her before I did was also in love with her.

"The unfortunate part of these delusions is that it makes it impossible to continue visiting the patient. If I had gone to see her regularly this crazy idea of hers would have been strengthened. In fact, it was because I saw that my calls were merely encouraging it that I stayed away."

Susan again sighed with relief. This, of course, explained what the girl had meant when she had said, "Go back on me, would you?" Indeed, it made pathetically clear all her remarks, and explained away her tears.

Poor little thing! How strange that one who did not look insane should harbour such odd delusions. Certainly the girl had not seemed mad. She had appeared a very ordinary person, save that she was prettier than the average woman. How sad! Susan's tender heart was touched at Miss Fuller's strange plight.

"Could I do anything for her?" she inquired timidly. "Money or anything, I mean? Or go to see her and take her something —flowers, perhaps, or books?"

The doctor smiled.

"You are indeed the fairy princess that I thought you the first night we met," he said ardently. "But, bless your darling little heart, there is nothing you can do for Doll Fuller. To see you would only remind her that she had made a little idiot of herself, and that would not be good for her. No, no; the only thing that I can do is to hand her over to Bollinger, the nerve man. I'll speak to him at the hospital tomorrow."

He crossed to his desk and made a note.

"I shan't forget now that I've written it down," he remarked casually, adding more thoughtfully: "But I shall have to make her understand, that she must put herself in Bollinger's care."

"That means that you won't be able to join me until late, doesn't it?" queried Susan regretfully.

"I'm afraid it does. Still, I can't neglect the poor little soul. A doctor has to think of his patients before he thinks of himself, or even of someone more precious to him than himself. It doesn't do to let a nervous patient get too down."

And he continued to tell her of the treatment that such cases required.

But as he spoke he watched her closely. He wanted to be certain that she believed his explanation of Doll Fuller's visit. When she had made it clear beyond all doubt that she had accepted his statements as facts, his expression became sorrowful, and he sighed a little and thus caused her to ask him why he seemed sad.

"It just hurt for a moment to see doubt in your eyes," he said; and at once she was all contrition. She flung her arms about him. She kissed him, tenderly at first, and then, when she felt the ardour that fired his blood communicate itself to her, passionately.

As he caressed the enraptured girl, like her he seemed lost to all but the feverish joy of the moment, but actually his brain had never been more alert. His mind was working with the swiftness of lightning. Susan would be his now, and for all time, if he willed it. He knew it; he was certain of it! And then no human being could take her from him. It meant making doubly sure of her.

But, no. He was sure of her, in any case. And it was important to him that he should enter the Carstairs family as the honoured, not the scapegrace, son-in-law. It was all important. Words were sufficient for the present.

"I wish we were married, Susan," he said in a low, thrilling voice. "I could make you even more certain then that poor Doll Fuller meant nothing to me. I could make you forget that there was such a person living, or that anybody existed in the whole world but me."

Gently he disengaged himself and stood up.

"It has got late, our tea-party, I'm afraid, has gone west, and I must see you home," he said, adding in the intimate tender tone she loved: "But, gosh, it's a sacrifice!"

"Only three weeks more, and then home will be wherever you are," said Susan, a quiver of emotion making her words unsteady. "Won't that be paradise? But before we go do, do please tell me that you forgive me absolutely. You understand that it was only because you are so precious to me?"

North smiled the delightful smile that had won him so many friends.

"Of course, darling! Don't ever give it another thought."

Susan sought to obey his injunction ever after, for the bare recollection of Doll Fuller's visit was painful. Thus lightly did she dismiss her meeting with the woman fated to play a vital part in a drama which was working slowly, relentlessly towards its climax.

Next week's issue which also contains a story of the Criminals' Confederation: and Sir Phillip Champion —see page 22) will bring the second instalment of this wonderfully gripping story. Deliberately has Dr. North laid his sinister plan; irresistibly it moves on, bearing with it the helpless, unknowing victims of the doctor's villainy, and even the doctor himself, to its final conclusion of logic and drama — puppets of fate entangled in a web of deception and death. This yarn will unfailingly grip you. Not a single instalment should be missed.

Printed and published every Thursday by the Proprietors, The Amalgamated Press, Ltd., The Fleetway House, Farringdon Street, London, E.C.4. Advertisement offices: The Fleetway House, Farringdon Street, London, E. C.4. Registered for transmission by Canadian Magazine Post. Subscription rates: Inland and Abroad, 11s. per annum; 5s. 6d. for six months. Sole Agents for Australia and New Zealand: Messrs. Gordon & Gotch, Ltd and for South Africa: Central News Agency, Ltd. — Saturday, December 26th, 1931.

THE ROUND TABLE

The Round Table

WHAT with the butting-in of one thing and another, we haven't really had a chance to discuss fully the subject I broached —and then had to switch over to another topic —the week before last.

It's a big subject, anyway, and, after all, a page is only a page, as the hotel reception clerk remarked scornfully to the chief door-porter. The subject, as you will remember, is the contest we had some little time ago on the question of "What I think of the 'U. J.,' " and the business of the meeting at the moment to discover just what members of the Round Table in the lump actually do think of it, and why, and how. Also, to decide what we're going to do about it.

Several things we have already debated; and, more to the point, acted on. Chief of your revelations was that you thought a whole lot of the old Criminals' Confederation and Mr. Reece. You said you'd like to have stories about them in the paper once again. O.K.! As you know, they've begun already, and, incidentally, the second one is due next week. They'll go on till you give the word to stop them.

From all the indications, though, I imagine that word will not be given. It is twelve years since the Reece series began, but so firm a grip have they, even after all this time, on the memories and affections of the old- timers, that there was a thumping majority who howled to have them back. There are no yarns like the old yarns apparently.

On this particular issue we have yet to hear the voice of the newcomers, the younger generation. Maybe they will prefer the characters who have arisen since the palmy days of Mr. Reece. If so, let them not hesitate to say so. What's the use of being able to sit in at the Round Table and not make a little speech sometimes, anyway?

But the betting at the moment is that they'll like him now as much as the older generation did then —and do now —especially when events develop in the Confederation's history. A big, world-circling organisation, it gave Sexton Blake and Coutts the biggest job of their lives, bar none. And as yet the stirring adventures it led them into have hardly got into their stride.

Other firm favourites who somehow lapsed from the limelight are Lobangu and Sir Richard (Spots) Loseley. Well, you're going to meet them once again, too, and that shortly. The first of a new epic concerning Blake, Lobangu, and Sir Richard, in Africa, will be in your hands in four issues from now. The author is Rex Hardinge — and if you've read previous yarns of the Dark Continent which he has written you're justified in expecting something great.

Other names which were greeted with acclamation and a demand for more were: Mademoiselle Roxane, George Marsden Plummer, Huxton Rymer, Waldo, Zenith, Splash Page, and various others who have ofttimes given you pleasure before. The result of your voting is that they will do so again. Just as often as we can give them all a fair turn, in fact.

Boiled down, your combined verdict undoubtedly was that you wanted more of the old favourites, and by a careful checking of all the answers received we know which of them you want, and how urgently you want them.

Naturally, your wishes are being translated into action —and the sort of yarns you prefer —without delay. The result —each issue will be of higher average appeal. You will be able to buy it "blind" each week, without knowing even what the story is, and yet know that the chances are it is more likely to please you than one previously published without the benefit of a mass vote to decide the most popular fare.

To turn to the opposite side of the picture.

American gang stuff has been popular in its day as a novelty. We in this peaceful isle wanted to see what hectic things they were getting up to in the States. Well, we have seen; and now, like Queen Victoria, we are not amused. Britishers have decided that, if gangsters and Prohibition bring about those results, America is welcome to gang rule, and can have a monopoly of it.

But certainly there was a fashion for gang yarns, prompted by curiosity of novelty, perhaps; and, being an up-to-date paper, UNION JACK supplied the demand while it lasted. But now, to all practical purposes, it's dead.

One other thing has come back in response to your edict —the Round Table. Again there was a majority in favour. Readers in great numbers went on record as saying that they always enjoyed the bright and matey conferences we used to have —and why not have them again?

Well, the Round Table's back, too, and will appear regularly unless there is such great demand for the space that it has to be postponed.

So, you see that we here at headquarters are out to make the Old Paper as nearly 100 per cent. welcome to you, individually and in the mass, as we possibly can.

We are doing —and will continue to do —our part. It's up to you to do yours. Everyone who reads this knows of somebody who would like the yarns we publish. Maybe he or she has enjoyed them in the past, and has somehow lapsed from the good habit. That someone is a prospective reader, and is eventually going to thank you for being reminded of the good stuff available in "U. J." every week for the modest price of 2d.

Think it over. It isn't much for you to do, and it's mainly because of such little services by keen readers in the past that Sexton Blake has become the world figure he is. If you like our yarns yourself, don't make a secret of it. Telling the news is the best service you can do your friends, and —

Your Editor

From Information Received

Murder with a Christmas Eve Climax —Prohibition Apologies — Prison Football.

The late Mr. JUSTICE KENNEDY.
His only murder trial was decided on Christmas Eve.

CLUES GIVEN AWAY *by a murderer gave a judge a most unhappy Christmas.*

A DIM, candle-lit court-room during the closing hours of Christmas Eve was the scene of one of the most dramatic murder trials in the records of British law.

At a time when the rest of the world was gaily making its last-minute preparations for the festivities of Yule; when parents were filling Christmas stockings and sleeping innocents were dreaming of Santa Claus; when shops and homes were gay with seasonable fare and bright with lights, a man's life or death was being decided in the shadowy old County Hall at Northampton, and a distressed, emotional judge was preparing to read, with blurred eyes, the words of the dread sentence of death.

The case was that of the murder of Annie Pritchard, in 1892. The trial of the prisoner, Andrew George MacRae, was the climax to a piece of dogged detective work which has hardly been excelled since.

Annie Pritchard's body was found by the roadside between Northampton and Rugby, wrapped in sacking. Attached to the sacking was a label bearing the name and address "E. M. Rae, Northampton." The owner of this name was discovered. He was a farmer living at Althorpe, who ran a stall for the selling of his bacon in the town, and was usually known as Edward MacRae. The police, after due investigation, were able to absolve him of any suspicion in the matter; the sack was merely one of many such in which his bacon was sold.

He had a brother, Andrew, and him, also, the police put under the microscope. Andrew had left his wife in Birmingham and was employed by Edward MacRae at the bacon stall in Northampton. Quiet inquiries were made there, and it was found that the wife was actually alive, in spite of any ideas to the contrary.

The body of the dead woman, which it was impossible to

identify, was therefore not that of Mrs. Andrew MacRae. Possible suspicion against her husband therefore lapsed, and at the inquest the verdict was "Murder by Some Person or Persons Unknown."

AND there the mystery would have remained, but for the astuteness of a Birmingham police officer, Detective Squires, who was one of those who had looked into the matter at the request of the Northampton police. It did not follow, according to his reasoning, that a wife might be the only woman a man wished to get rid of; and the label on the sacking was a clue not to be ignored. Methodically, he set about his own inquiries.

Approaching the suspect's wife in Birmingham once more, he soon got a clue. The MacRaes had been on friendly terms with their next-door neighbours, the Pritchards, and Andrew was often in and out of their house. Annie, one of the daughters, had lately gone to America, said Mrs. MacRae, having just married an old lover named Anderson. Nobody of the family had been present at the wedding, however. The news had come by letter, from Liverpool, on the eve of the trip, and was all the more surprising because it was known that Annie had not so much as seen the man for at least eighteen months. Since this letter no word had been heard of her.

At just about this time, the detective found, Andrew MacRae had also left Birmingham and gone to Northampton to work for his brother. That was at the end of March.

Then came a red-hot clue. A Northampton secondhand clothes dealer came forward who had bought from a man a parcel of women's clothes which, like the body of the unknown woman, were wrapped in a sack bearing the name of Rae. This transaction had taken place early in August, a few days after the body had been discovered on the seventh, but it was not till nearly a month afterwards that the information came to the police.

The secondhand dealer was able to produce one of the articles. It was a nightdress, and Detective Squires took it to Birmingham, where *it was promptly identified by Lizzie Pritchard as the property of her sister Annie.*

On September 3rd, Andrew MacRae was arrested.

EVIDENCE was piling up now that the police, with Squires leading the hunt, were hot on the scent. Various articles in the prisoner's possession were recognised as once having been Annie Pritchard's;

and a search of Edward MacRae's warehouse, in which Andrew spent a good deal of his time, revealed burned bones and several brown hairs from the head of a woman.

Probing into the past, the police soon turned up other damaging matters. They found that Andrew MacRae and Annie Pritchard —her photo was identified by the landlady —had taken lodgings at the house of a Mrs. Pilkington. They moved from there, and MacRae next became the tenant of a Mrs. Philpot. *But he arrived there alone.*

A man testified that Annie Pritchard (whom he recognised from a photograph) had come to him in Northampton and asked him to post a letter for her in Liverpool. (The letter about the alleged trip to America.) Various other people gave evidence of his purchase of lime; of his having given away surplus lime which he could not use; of seeing thick, oily smoke coming from the warehouse chimney; and of the purchase from MacRae of various articles bearing the dead woman's initials. Also, the railway company were able to show that Annie Pritchard's luggage was sent from Birmingham to Northampton on the date when she was supposed to be going to Liverpool.

These separate strands of evidence remorselessly spun themselves into a rope strong enough to hang a man far less clever than the clumsy Andrew MacRae, who had scattered damning clues right and left since the commencement of his crime. It is almost inconceivable that a murderer would be careless enough to leave a label giving his name both on the body of his victim and on the wrapping of the victim's property, the mere selling of which was dangerous enough in itself. The neglect of other precautions in covering his tracks was almost equally foolish.

After a tense battle of legal experts which finally opened on December 20th, and in which the ground was fought over foot by foot, the closing scenes were reached in the dusk of Christmas Eve.

Mr. Justice Kennedy had never presided at a murder trial before. He was known as too tender-hearted a judge for the ordeal of passing a death sentence, and the task of impartially sifting the evidence and of instructing the jury in his summing-up must have been more than usually severe for him. The candle-light glinted on the pallid faces of the packed spectators against the dark panelled walls of the old building as, in an atmosphere of taut emotion, the judge bade the jury retire to consider their verdict.

And as they withdrew one of the candles guttered and died, casting a corner of the chamber into deeper shadow and filling the watchers' hearts with a sense of ill-omen.

It was justified by the outcome. The facts were all against the man in the dock. The verdict was "Guilty."

With moist eyes, and in a shaky voice, the judge read out the words of the sentence which he could not trust himself to repeat unaided, and which he had written out beforehand in expectation of the result. Andrew MacRae was duly hanged in the following January.

But the judge, whose sensitive soul had been harrowed not only by the ordeal, but by the contrast between the dread scene and the season of peace and good will, never tried another murder case.

READY-MADE REGRETS for "the morning after" are Prohibition's latest prank.

PROHIBITION in America, the cause which has produced many strange effects, added another to its list when it brought about a new form of Christmas-card.

A repentant reveller, waking on a grey morning-after-the-night-before with a nasty taste in his mouth and a hazy remorse in his heart, is apt to dimly realise that the bootleg liquor at the party had been too potent for his personality.

In other words, the stuff had such a kick in it that he strongly suspects that the good manners for which he is renowned were then conspicuous entirely by their absence; he remembers, with a shudder of shame, that his baser self had taken charge and carried on outrageously.

He will have to apologise to his hostess. Nothing simpler! There are others like that, too, and they are catered for by a new form of postal apology. He merely has to go to the stationer's and buy the most suitable of a selection of printed cards, on which he indicates his particular sins and sends to his hostess instead of making a laborious apology in words.

Here is a specimen:

Mr. . ...

sincerely apologises for his most regrettable lapses while a guest

at your party on

and wishes to ask your forgiveness of following breaches of good manners:

Staggering into hostess or other guests.

Smashing furniture.

Squirting soda-water on ceiling.

Striking hostess with bottle.

Using gramophone records as boomerangs.

Refusing to go home.

Excessive argument.

Criticising hostess' mother.

Doubtless, the hostess, accepting his frank admission of, say, criticising her mother, realises when she sees the rest of the list, that it might have been worse.

He might have struck her —the hostess herself —with a bottle.

The football ground inside the walls of Sing Sing, with a practice match in progress.

HOME MATCHES ONLY are on the fixture list of Sing Sing Prison's football team at present.

But perhaps they're hoping for away dates, too.

PROBABLY one of the main attractions on the Christmas entertainments programme at Sing Sing Prison will be another football match.

That is, if the Sing Sing First XI. can get a suitable date fixed up. It'll have to be a home match, of course. They haven't been able to arrange any away dates as yet. And they won't be able to play even a home match if there's a killing. But we'll come to that in a minute.

Oh, no, it's no leg-pull; the convicts in this world famous prison of New York State have had a football team for some time. Or teams, rather; they have played inter-prison matches until just lately, but Warden Lawes —almost as famous for his advanced humanitarian treatment of convicts as is the prison where he practises it —started something entirely new in the way of prison programmes when he permitted a picked convicts' team to play one from the outside.

It was a great day! The home crowd beat the visitors 33 goals to nil!

The Sing-Songsters (if that's the name they're going to adopt) are a strong team. They welcome all comers, but prefer military or police teams. "Alabama" Pitts is the skipper, a husky lad who learned his football in the U.S. Navy, and something less innocent elsewhere; hence his present address. The coach, "Red End" Hope, is being detained in consequence of a bit of kidnapping when he was last at liberty.

It is safe to say that no such football match has been seen before. The gate was 700. These were specially privileged visitors admitted from outside —and every one of them was searched for arms. The precaution was necessary enough, of course, on account of possible confederates smuggling firearms to the "cons." and a riot or prison-break resulting.

Besides the 700 outsiders, 2,300 of the home team's supporters lined up to cheer. Unseen by either crowd were the machine-guns and the guards on the walls overlooking the ground. More in evidence were the movie and news-camera men with their apparatus, and microphones which carried the noises of the match, and the running commentary, to patients in the prison hospital and others who could not be present.

The football ground inside the walls of Sing Sing, with a practice match in progress.

THE prison band was on the spot to play the teams out, and the prisoners' mascot was also amongst those present. A humorous touch, this. It was a black pony painted with white stripes, the idea being, according to some, that it represented a zebra. But others, rightly or wrongly, urged that the colour scheme was emblematical of the old-time black-and-white-striped convict uniform. Anyway, the mascot got a great reception as it paraded before the match amidst the cheers of the 3,000 onlookers and the blaring of the band, and so did the warden's little daughter, who led it.

The opposing team was that of the Ossining Naval Militia, and the Sing Sing captain's orders were not to be too rough with them. To give them their due, the home team played a thoroughly clean game, but nevertheless wiped the visitors up 33 —nil, as stated.

We repeat, it was a great day, and it would be apt, though perhaps inaccurate, to say the convicts are talking about it yet. The reason they are probably not is that at time of writing, they are booked to play the Port Jervis Police XI., and they are deep in a discussion of prospects.

The games, by the way, take place on Sundays, and so good is the moral effect of them on the men "inside" that they will probably be continued for the remainder of the season, and resumed next.

But it was touch and go whether they ever began at all. Warden Lawes had permitted the inter-prison matches for some months, only finally deciding to sanction the games with visiting teams in November last. The first one, with the Naval Militia, was scheduled for the 15th of the month, but on the 13th, the Friday before, some unknown convict fatally stabbed another convict named Schoonmaker.

This murder naturally upset the serenity of the sporting atmosphere, and Warden Lawes forthwith forbade the practice games, and considered cancelling also the big game on the Sunday. It was probably a very wise decision when he relented and allowed the arrangements to stand. After all, there is far less chance of murders happening in a prison where men can discuss last week's or next week's game, instead of brooding on killing.

Meantime, watch the Sing Sing fixture list. They're a tough

bunch, and should make a good showing. The only trouble is, if they attain League status —or its American equivalent —how are their supporters going to be present to cheer them to victory at their away matches?

LEWIS E. LAWES,
the man who sanctioned Sing Sing's football.